GHOST
SHADOWS

THOMAS M. MALAFARINA

GHOST SHADOWS

For information about special discounts for bulk purchases, please contact
Sunbury Press, Inc. Wholesale Dept. at (855) 338-8359 or
orders@sunburypress.com.

To request one of our authors for speaking engagements or book signings,
please contact Sunbury Press, Inc. Publicity Dept. at
publicity@sunburypress.com.

FIRST SUNBURY PRESS EDITION
Printed in the United States of America
March 2013

Trade Paperback ISBN: 978-1-62006-193-0
Mobipocket format (Kindle) ISBN: 978-1- 62006-194-7
ePub format (Nook) ISBN: 978-1-62006-195-4

Published by:
Sunbury Press
Mechanicsburg, PA
www.sunburypress.com

Mechanicsburg, Pennsylvania   USA

This book is dedicated to my amazing wife Joanne for all of her love, kindness, inspiration and patience; and especially for her willingness to put up with my writing all of these horrible stories and still be willing to sleep next to me at night.

Table of Contents

Introduction

In late 2012, I was putting together a group of short stories for possible publication in early 2013 by Sunbury Press. The collection was an eclectic assortment of various stories, which did not really fit into a specific theme although the genre was most definitely suspenseful horror. Some of the stories were ghost stories; some were a mix of technology and the supernatural; some were demonic in nature, some more psychological thrillers, and some didn't quite fit into any particular category. A few were somewhat short while others had become quite long.

Several of the stories were brand new, having never been previously published anywhere and were written specifically for this collection. A couple of them previously appeared as part of other multi-author anthologies by a variety of publishers but have never been published in any of my Sunbury Press collections. Two of them appeared in a special Sunbury collection called *Malafarina Maleficarum Volume II*. Each of them has been revised, reworked, and rewritten by me for the purposes of this collection.

That being said, I was in need of a title and cover for this new collection and I still needed a few more stories to finish it off. At the same time I had started two or three new novels which for now will remain secret as I hope to finish and publish them in the near future. What to do . . . what to do . . . . Then the inspiration came to me unexpectedly one day in December 2012 when my wife, JoAnne, came home from work with a photograph she took with her iPhone of a shadow on a window at her place of employment.

In October 2012, her department and several others in the company where she worked had moved into a newly renovated office building in the town a few miles down the road from her main office. Apparently sometime, perhaps while the renovation of the building was taking place, no one really knows for sure, a bird must have flown against one of the windows, broken its neck, and died. Since that time, the outsides of the windows had not been cleaned.

One day in early December when JoAnne was getting ready to leave for the day the sun was just at the right position to strike the glass and allow the image, which is shown on the front of the cover of this book, to appear. We assume the image resulted from the collection of dust stuck to the bird's body transferring from the bird to the window at the time of impact. For months it had gone unnoticed until just the right set of natural conditions existed for it to make its presence known. Since the initial photograph was taken she has tried to numerous times photograph it using our Nikon 35mm, but the conditions have never been good enough to get a proper shot. Even though I wanted a black and white photo on the front cover I put the original color version of the image on the back cover.

Anyway, after she saw the photo, she emailed it to me and I immediately loved it as she knew I would. I was inspired and knew I would use it in one of my future works but that it might take a day or so for me to figure out exactly what I would want to do with it. In the meantime, she sent it to the Weather Channel Web site and they posted it up on their animal photo section where it received some nice comments. We also shared it with our Facebook friends to many positive reviews.

JoAnne told me some of her coworkers said the image almost looked like an angel to them while others thought it looked like a demon. One person said it appeared that the bird had left an imprint of its soul on the window. Hearing those impressions I was instantly motivated. I realized I had found the answer to my short story collection title issue. The title, *Ghost Shadows* jumped right into my mind and made perfect reference not only to the bird's shadow in the photo but to the ghostly shadows I hope my writing casts upon the minds and souls of my readers. I was also then inspired to write a short story about the image based on what JoAnne had told me about the various interpretations of the shadow, which became the short story "Ghost Shadow." Before the end of December 2012 I had the cover completed, two thirds of the stories in place, and the remaining stories laid out and ready to write and or rework. My goal was to have a collection of thirteen tales ready for Sunbury Press for publication by March 2013.

My publisher, Lawrence Knorr, had the great idea to release the collection on 3/13/13 at 13:13 hrs. I loved the idea and began to work my backside off to meet my self-imposed deadline, which I obviously did, as you are now reading the results. *Ghost Shadows* is a not so nice collection of thirteen haunting tales that I hope you enjoy as much as you have enjoyed my other works. I look forward to continuing to bring you the best horror stories my twisted little mind can conjure up for you in the years to come.

Thomas M. Malafarina, March 2013

Ghost Shadow

Inspired by a photo by JoAnne Malafarina

*Thoughts are the shadows of our feelings—always
darker, emptier and simpler.*
— Friedrich Nietzsche

*I do not say think as I think, but think in my way. Fear
no shadows, least of all in that great specter of personal
unhappiness which binds half the world to orthodoxy.*
— Thomas Huxley

"Thank God this day is finally over," Jill Christopher
said as she laboriously raised herself up from her desk
chair and did a slow, much needed stretch. It was 5:05 on
Wednesday afternoon, December 12, 2012. The day had
been a hectic one, as her workdays often tended to be, but
this one had been a bit more strange than most. In
between trying to talk to clients on the phone and
straightening out billing errors she was barraged with
emails and visits from coworkers; the subject of both being
the fact that the day was 12/12/2012.

There seemed to be a great fervor in the world about
the end of the Mayan calendar coming on December 21
and supposedly many people believed this meant the world
would come to an end on that date as well. As a result,
some people assumed the coincidence of the triple-twelve
occurrence in the date had to have some significant
meaning as well. But as far as Jill was concerned it meant
nothing but one more day she had to try to do the work of
three people on her own.

She shut off her computer and turned to leave the office
when she noticed something on the window behind her. Jill
had no idea why she hadn't seen it before. Her department,
along with several others, had only moved into the newly

4

renovated office building in October and every day she left at the same time and followed the same routine, yet she had never seen such a sight previously. There on her window was the image of what appeared to be a bird. The thing was perfectly formed and looked almost as if someone had sketched a picture of bird on the outside of her second floor window. But it was not a sketch: it was an actually image of a bird on the glass. She was amazed by the clarity of the shadow. A thought immediately ran through her mind. "Ghost shadow," she heard a small voice say inside of her. But she knew there were no ghosts or such things and that no matter how perfectly the image appeared its formation was based on science rather than the supernatural.

She took three steps to the left and the image all but disappeared. Only a barely recognizable remnant remained. Then she took two steps to the right of her original position with similar results. Only when she stood at that one spot was she able to see the image in its entirety. She reached over to her desk and pulled off two long strips of tape. She found the optimal viewing position once more and made an 'X' on the floor with the tape.

Next, using her smart phone, Jill snapped several pictures of the image she saw on the window. She checked the pictures on her phone and was thrilled with the quality. She immediately emailed one of the best shots to her husband, Todd, who was a horror fiction writer. She knew he would enjoy seeing the picture and was certain it would stimulate his creative juices. He would likely create a short story based on the picture for all she knew. She could hear movement in the cubicle next to hers and realized her coworker, Marie, had not yet left for the day.

"Marie? Are you still here?" Jill asked.

Marie hesitated for a moment then replied with a bit of hesitation in her voice. "Um . . . yeah . . . I'm still here. So is Josie. I hope you don't have something urgent for me to do. I was hoping to get out of here on time tonight."

"No. Nothing like that," Jill replied. "I just wanted to show you something over here. Bring Josie with you. This is too cool to miss."

When Marie and Josie rounded the corner of Jill's cubical both wearing curious expressions they found Jill standing on the tape 'X' on the floor and staring at the window. Without looking at them she gestured for them to come closer and said, "Quick, stand on this 'X' and look at the back window."

Marie looked strangely at Jill but did as instructed and her face illuminated with an expression of complete amazement. "Oh my word!" Marie exclaimed. "Just look at that . . . it's . . . it's incredible!" Marie was a large woman of about sixty-three with curly gray hair and perpetually smiling eyes. Those eyes were now staring at the window with astonishment. She said, "I don't think I've ever seen anything like this before."

"What is it?" Josie asked, standing off to the side and unable to see the image. "What are you looking at?"

"A bird, I think." Marie said. "I think it's some sort of image of a bird on the window. I wonder how it got there."

Jill explained, "I think what may have happened is a bird must have flown into the window sometime and most likely broke its neck and died. Bird feathers are oily and collect dust and dirt particles. My guess is the image is a result of that oily dust residue sticking to the window at the time of impact. It probably has been there for months but for some reason the sun must be at just the right position for us to see it today."

"But it's so perfect, so complete!" Marie said. "It's as if the bird's very soul was imprinted on the glass."

"I want to see it!" Josie exclaimed. Josie was a young woman in her mid-twenties. She had gotten divorced from her alcoholic and abusive husband a year earlier. She had grown up with a father who was also a drunk who beat her mother and had unfortunately followed in her mother's footsteps. Since becoming single Josie embarked on a mission to find spiritual enlightenment. She had experimented with numerology, Hinduism, Buddhism, and most recently Christianity. In fact she was currently a member of a right wing fundamentalist Christian church and had become "born again" just a month earlier.

From the way Josie spoke of her church, both Jill and Marie felt this church was more of a cult than a above board religious organization. They tried to warn her about such groups but had to tread softly as to not hurt her feelings or risk alienating their coworker with her fragile and needy psyche. Plus the both knew in the modern workplace, negative discussions about someone's race, religion, or such were grounds for disciplinary action, up to an including termination.

Josie stood on the 'X' and stared at the window transfixed. "Oh my sweet Lord!" Josie said. She had been using that expression a lot since her conversion. "It's . . . it's . . . incredible! It's amazing!"

"Yes it is very interesting, Josie, but it's just bird dust." Jill said trying to keep Josie's growing fervor under control. She knew her coworker too well and could tell she was getting overzealous at seeing the image. "It's simply a collection of dust on the surface of the glass."

Marie interjected, "Looks like the bird left his soul on the window to me." She was not helping matters.

"You're both wrong!" Josie said. "It's not a bird or a bird's soul. Look at it closely. It's the image of an angel. It's a sign! It's a true miracle!"

"Don't be silly," Jill said, doing her best to dampen Josie's enthusiasm somewhat. What she really wanted to say was "don't be ridiculous" or "don't be such an idiot."

Josie said even louder, "I'm telling you . . . it's a message from God! Today is 12-12-12; that is significant. It means something. Can't you feel it?" She pulled out her own smart phone and snapped several pictures.

Jill realized Josie was mixing her study of numerology with her Christianity and putting undeserved significance on the date. Things were starting to get out of hand. She had to do something.

"Josie. Relax." Jill pleaded. "It's just a bird. Nothing more. The bird is long dead and it's just a dust shadow."

Josie asked, "Well if it's a dead bird, where's the body? I'll bet if I go downstairs and look out the double doors to the back patio there won't be any signs of a bird."

Jill was beginning to lose patience with Josie, "Look, Josie. In the first place I have no idea how long ago this happened. We've only been in the building for two months. It could have happened anytime. Maybe one of the construction workers disposed of the bird's body. Who knows? There's a forest no more than one hundred feet behind this building, maybe scavengers drug it into the woods and picked it clean. We probably will never know what happened to it."

"That's because nothing happened to it." Jill insisted. "There was no body because there was no bird. This miracle was an imprint on the window that I was meant to see. I am to be the deliverer of the message. God has spoken to me through this angelic sign."

Just when Jill was about to completely lose her temper and call Josie an out of control whacko they heard a booming voice from behind them. "What the hell is going on over here?" It was their company general manager, Sid Emerich. "I'm trying to run a business here. What's all this crazy talk about angels and miracles?" Sid walked over to the small group of women, and as he did, Jill saw several others enter her work area. There was Amy Jamison from accounts payable, Cindy Smith from HR and that strange new Goth-looking girl Sandy or Sarah or something like that from the IT department.

Jill didn't care much for her dark clothing, heavy makeup, and various facial piercings, not to mention her tattoos that could not be properly hidden with her clothing. She didn't feel this was proper office attire and could not begin to imagine how this young woman made it through the interview process and somehow managed to get hired.

"Mr. Emerich! It's a miracle!" The overly excited Josie shouted while waving her left arm high in the air and clutching her cross necklace with the right. "God has sent us a sign; an angelic symbol on the window!"

Jill stepped forward in a last attempt to try to smooth over the escalating confrontation. "Sorry about all this commotion, Mr. Emerich. It's really nothing at all, just the image on the window; a dust shadow from some bird that must have flown into the glass. That's all it is."

"Let me see this!" Emerich said, shoving Josie aside. Like the others Emerich stood directly on the 'X' and looked at the window. Without showing any emotion, Emerich simply turned to the group and said, "Jill is correct. It is just a dusty shadow. Nothing more."

"I think it's an angel; in fact I know it is." Josie insisted, "This is a sign from God, Hallelujah! Praise be to the Lord on high! Jesus is coming and all you sinners better be ready!"

Emerich fumed with rage and shouted, "That's entirely enough of that crazy cackling from you young lady! There'll be no more of such idiotic gibberish permitted in my office! Is that clear?" Emerich had a habit of stressing the importance of all of his proclamations by ending them with the phrase "Is that clear?" or "Have I made myself perfectly clear?" or some other similar variation. It usually got people to snap to attention but didn't seem to have the same effect on Josie.

"How dare you blaspheme the Lord!" Josie shouted right back at him. "And how dare you criticize me and my beliefs. You are creating a hostile work environment and discriminating against me because of my religious beliefs. And that, Mr. Emerich, is illegal."

Josie stared directly at Cindy Smith, who looked as if she would rather have been anywhere than where she was. "Cindy. You tell him. You are our Human Resources Manager, or at least you're supposed to be. Tell him he can't criticize me or threaten me because of my religious choices."

Cindy looked dumfounded as her eyes nervously darted between Josie and Emerich. Eventually, those eyes stopped at Emerich and she shrugged her shoulders as if to say, "She's absolutely right, boss. Our hands are tied here."

In the meantime, Sarah the Goth girl had taken a few more steps into the area and following behind her was Josie's boss, Phil Ralston.

Emerich's face reddened with anger at the realization that he could do nothing to stop Josie's outlandish behavior and he shouted "Fine! Believe whatever the hell you want to believe. But this is a place of business not a revival tent. And it's the end of the workday for most of you, so I strongly suggest you all go home and we will all start fresh tomorrow morning."

"That's fine with me," Josie shouted right back at him, "But I'm warning you, Mr. Emerich, if you have anyone wash that miraculous sign off the window, I will sue you personally as well as this company for religious persecution and for creating a hostile work environment."

Emerich looked as if his head were about to explode and Jill thought he might actually reach out and wrap his hands around Josie and strangle her to death. But instead he looked over at Cindy Smith who slowly shook her head, warning him he had better back down and keep his cool. Without another word, Emerich turned and stormed out of the area grabbing Phil Ralston by the arm and leading him away from the group.

They went into Phil's office and Emerich slammed the door shut shouting with uncontrolled anger, "That little holy rolling bitch works for you is that right, Ralston?"

"Y—ye—yes, Mr. Emerich. She does," Ralston replied realizing he was about to be put into a very unpleasant situation.

"Starting first thing tomorrow," Emerich bellowed, "you have a new top priority. I want you to start collecting paper on that little bible thumping psycho. If she forgets to dot an 'i'—document it. If she forgets to cross a 't'—document it. Every time she says one word to one of her coworkers about religion, God, or miracles, I want it documented. If she farts or burps or sneezes I want it down on paper. By then end of next month I want that mouthy bitch fired! Is that clear?"

Ralston tried to stand up for Josie to the best of his terrified ability. "But . . . but, Mr. Emerich. Josie is a good worker, one of the best I have. She's been through a lot in her personal life and still manages to do a good day's work for the company. I think asking me to fire her just because she got a bit overzealous today is somewhat rash, don't you think?"

"No, I most certainly do not think," Emerich shouted. "She has got to go. And as her supervisor it is your job to make it happen." Then he looked oddly at Ralston and suggested, "You don't mean to tell me you and that Josie are playing 'slap and tickle' are you, Ralston? You know how I feel about my mangers dipping their pens in the company ink."

"No. Absolutely not, Mr. Emerich. I would never—I have never . . ." Ralston stammered. The truth was, Ralston was only about ten years older than Josie and his wife had divorced him a year or so earlier. And he was quite attracted to Josie, despite her idiosyncrasies. Although he could not start a relationship with her, he did his best to take care of her and watch over her on the job.

Emerich said, "Good thing, Ralston. Because unless you want to join her among the ranks of the unemployed you had better find a way to get rid of her before the end of the month. Do I make myself perfectly clear?"

"Yes sir, Mr. Emerich," Ralston said, "I understand." But Phil Ralston didn't understand. Under normal circumstances he disliked Sid Emerich but today he despised the man for what he was forcing Phil to do.

"Now go back there and break up that mob. Send them all home and maybe after a good night's sleep all of this nonsense will die down," Emerich said.

Reluctantly, Phil Ralston did as instructed and unhappily made his way down the hall toward Jill's cubicle. To his surprise, when he got back to the area everyone was gone except for that new girl Sarah who was staring at the window and tucking her smart phone into her coat pocket.

"Well," Ralston said trying to sound as unconcerned as possible, "I suppose I should take a look at this bird shadow that is causing so much commotion."

The girl did not reply. She walked silently past him and as he took his place on the 'X', just as she turned the corner he heard her say to herself, "It's not a bird, and not an angel either. At least not a heavenly angel."

Ralston thought the remark to be a bit peculiar but chose to ignore it. As he saw the image of the bird appear on the window he said, "Remarkable! It's almost perfect in every way."

Sarah walked out of the building heading for her car. She held onto her smart phone tightly in her coat pocket. Sarah had gotten plenty of good shots of the image with her phone. She knew in her heart it was no bird shadow and most certainly was no angel; but it was a sign. And it was not a sign from Heaven; but from Hell. Sarah recognized a sign from the Dark One, her master, when she saw it. Today was 12-12-12 and Satan had chosen to make her aware of his coming. She was honored to be the chosen one; the messenger to deliver the news of his coming to his disciples.

That night the Internet was a very busy place indeed. Jill decided to send her copy of the photo to the Weather Channel, which posted it in their animal photos section. She was thrilled that it was chosen and told all of her Facebook friends about it.

But she was not the only one spreading the news of the image. Josie had sent a copy of the picture to her church's website where it was viewed by hundreds of parishioners. Plus she was going to email the image to all of her friends and relatives as well as post it on her own Facebook page, proclaiming the coming of the Lord. Likewise, Sarah spread the word through the various forms of social media she and her group of worshipers regularly used that she was the messenger of the Dark Lord and that the seventh seal had been broken announcing the coming of Satan. The result was that by midnight virtually everyone in the area had seen the image on the window and each had their own interpretations of what it might mean.

By the next morning, Jill had all but forgotten about the ghost shadow. It had been interesting and unique but as she drove to her job that morning, all that was on her mind was the mountain of work waiting for her at the office. It waited for her every day and never seemed to get any smaller. That was why she was caught completely off guard when she got close to the office and saw hundreds of cars parked for more than a mile along both sides of the highway leading to her office. She also noticed several news vans and trucks and saw camera crews walking around to the back side of the office building. She looked up and was surprised to see a news helicopter hovering above the back of the building. She wondered: What in the world was going on?

Jill slowly navigated through the sea of pedestrians eventually making it to her assigned parking space. She was thankful security managed to at least keep the cars on the highway and out of the company parking lot. As she approached the front door she picked up snippets of conversations and her heart thudded in her chest as she realized what was happening and the potential ramifications to her.

It was the ghost shadow, that image of the bird on the window. She had been the first one to see it. She had sent it to the Weather Channel and they had posted it on their website. Was it possible that the picture had gone viral overnight? If so that meant that thousands or millions of people had seen the picture. As she walked up the stairs to her second floor cubical she prayed that she was wrong and that all these people might not be there because of her stupid posting. She wondered if Mr. Emerich would blame this on her and maybe fire her for it. Her gut clenched when she thought about it. For her to get fired in this crappy economy would be devastating. Jill felt as if she might pass out.

Things did not seem much better when she turned the corner to her cubical and saw Sid Emerich, Phil Ralston, and a few other senior staff members standing by the window looking down into the back of the building. Even from her location Jill could see hundreds of people had filled the area behind the office building. She heard Emerich say, "She should be terminated immediately for this!"

Jill's stomach sank. Her worst fear had suddenly become a reality—and because of that stupid picture. She had no idea what she and Todd would do once she was out of work. She took an involuntary step backward around the corner so she could still hear their conversation without being seen. She heard her immediate supervisor, Phil Ralston say, "I have to agree with you on this, Sid. I suppose they both have go."

Both? Jill wondered. Who else were they talking about?

"Most definitely," Emerich said, "Both that holy roller Josie as well as that new girl with the dark clothes; that devil worshipping tramp, Sarah. And the sooner the better.

Jill suddenly felt a surge of relief. They weren't after her; they weren't going to shoot the messenger. Apparently, Josie and Sarah had done something to cause the media circus, which apparently was occurring behind the building.

"I've had my secretary put in a call to both the local and state police. They should be arriving shortly. In the meantime, I'm going downstairs and put a stop to this once and for all," Emerich said. "And I want you all to come with me as a show of force and solidarity." Jill peeked around the corner and saw the four members of Emerich's staff look at him, then each other with uncertainty. She didn't know what was happening out back but it was clear that none of Emerich's staff wanted to be part of it.

Emerich turned to head down followed by his reluctant managers. Jill ducked into an empty office just in time not to be seen. She figured she had somehow been lucky enough this time and there was no reason for them to see her and possibly be reminded that it was she who first saw the image. Out of sight, out of mind, she thought.

When they had all passed by and were a safe distance down the hall she ducked around the corner and walked cautiously toward the window where the ghost shadow was faintly visible in the morning sun. She found it curiously odd how she had worked near that window for several months and never saw the image yet now that she had seen it once she couldn't un-see it. True, it was not as prominent or recognizable as it had been the previous evening, but she could still make out its faint image.

As she got closer to the window, she saw a sight she could hardly believe. The entire back lot of the building from the back entrance to the forest edge was a sea of people; hundreds of them. They all appeared to be excited, if not agitated to the point of hysteria.

When she looked closer she could see the crowd seemed to be divided into two distinct groups. On the right side of the crowd were people wearing crosses and dressed in bright colors. Some were even dress in robes and vestments, resembling a heavenly choir. They were shouting various religious things such as Halleluiah and the like. Some were singing songs of praise. Some carried gold grosses mounted on wooden poles and others had carried hand-made signs reading such slogans as "Jesus is Coming," "Repent," and "The End Is Near."

A few were shirtless despite the December cold, and were beating their own backs bloody with long knotted ropes and thin tree branches. Jill believed the practice was called self-flagellation or something like that. She had read about it once but had never seen it before. After today, she hoped to never see it again.

The members of the left side of the crowd were the antithesis of those on the right. These people wore dark clothing; primarily leather, spiked with shiny silver studs. Jill had never see so many different types of body piercings or tattoos in her life. It was like being front row at a heavy metal concert. Some of these people also carried signs with slogans like "Prepare for the Coming Of Satan," and "The Dark Master Approaches." At the front of the crowd dressed in a much more sinister type of dark clothing than she had ever worn to work was Sarah, raising her fist high in the air and angrily shouting something indiscernible through the thick glass. Jill saw that to the right, Josie stood at the front angrily shouting something back at Sarah.

In fact, it appeared to Jill that both sides of the crowd closest to each other were shouting angrily back and forth. Suddenly it was clear what had happened and why Emerich wanted to fire the two women. Both of them must have gone home the previous evening and began spreading the word and copies of the photo to their friends and fellow believers, each interpreting the image in a way that best served their own belief system. And this flash mob, this pilgrimage of sorts was the result.

Although Jill was no scholar in the field of human behavior, she knew instinctively that no good could come of these two groups with such opposite beliefs being put into a stressful situation so close to each other. Each group was convinced that the image on the window was a sign from their chosen god and that they were right and the other group was wrong. Even through the thick insulated glass of the window, Jill could hear the constant buzz of the multitude of voices growing even louder, blending together into a dull roar. She could see the angry, hateful expressions on the faces of both sides as they shouted and chided each other. Jill felt as if she were standing on the rim of a volcano waiting for it to blow.

Behind the crowd were the members of the media with cameras and microphones watching and waiting. Jill could tell they, too, knew something bad was about to happen. But instead of trying to do something to calm people down they seemed to be studying the crowd and panting with anticipation like swarming sharks smelling blood in the water.

Suddenly she felt a vibration under her feet and realized the back double doors of the office had opened. She heard the booming baritone of Sid Emerich trying futilely to be heard over the ever-increasing din of the crowd. She could not make out what Emerich was saying, but knowing Sid he was ordering everyone to disperse immediately and leave his property.

As the voices grew louder and the tempers began to grow in kind Jill noticed some of the zealots on both sides who were closest to each other begin to push and shove each other. She didn't know if the reason for the shoving was to try to get a closer look at the image on the window or if it was simply a result of their disdain for each other. All the while, Emerich continued to shout back at them and the press continued photographing and filming waiting for the imminent explosion of human emotion.

Then it happened. No one would ever know for sure which side did it or even why but suddenly from the back center of the crowd where both sides blended reluctantly together a large rock was thrown, striking Sid Emerich hard on the left temple. He dropped immediately to the ground—dead. Soon another rock flew and hit Phil Ralston square in the eye. He shouted in pain and anger as his hand reflexively reached up to cover the punctured orb, which oozed blood and vitreous matter, and which would never see again. That was when the trouble began.

Jill watched helplessly from her window, staring through the image of the bird shadow as the two sides erupted into a storm of violence. Like ancient warriors on the field of battle the two opposing crowds merged together in a flurry of swinging fists as what seemed like gallons of blood spilled to the ground. Moans of pain and thumping of flesh against flesh were everywhere as the madness spread through the crowd like wildfire.

When it was all over, thirty-two people were dead, including both Josie and Sarah. More than one hundred and twenty people were badly injured with seventy-five of them requiring hospitalization for major injuries. Several days later seven more would die at the hospital from complications suffered on that day. Some of the injuries and deaths were a direct result of blows received during the scuffle, and sadly many were simply trampled to death by the surging crowd. The entire event was caught on film by the media who were safely out of the zone of violence, yet the melee was so chaotic that no charges could be filed on anyone. The press had back row seats at a visage that could only be described as mankind at its worst.

Later, after the state and local police had regained control of the situation and the dead and wounded were removed, Cindy Smith from the HR department walked through the building checking to see how many workers had been wise enough to stay inside and were still safe. Cindy found Jill sitting on the floor leaning against the glass window staring up at the ghost shadow. She seemed to be in shock and her lips were moving as if quietly repeating something over and over.

Cindy asked, "Jill, honey. Are you all right?" Jill did not respond but kept staring at the image and apparently mumbling the same elusive phrase. Cindy knew as long as she lived, she would never forget the glazed look of despair on Jill's face, or the words she repeated. Jill had been saying, "Sometimes a bird is just a bird."

Automotive Graveyard

Inspired by a photo by Lawrence Knorr

*No trait is more justified than revenge in the
right time and place.*

—Meir Kahane

Like monstrous rusting hulks, the ancient shells of
what once were noble classic automobiles now lay hidden
from the prying eyes of the civilized world by a thick
creeping blanket of overwhelming forest undergrowth.
Dozens of trees sized from meager saplings to full grown
majestic behemoths towered far above the ground,
entwining themselves in and around the corroding,
formerly-mechanized cadavers.

Dense, impenetrable snaking vines of kudzu and other
such equally aggressive vegetation likewise knotted
themselves so cripplingly about the machines as to make
them virtually indiscernible. The upper halves of the
largest trees seemed to literally propagate upward from
deep within the mountainous piles of greenery-encased
metal. Many trees had collapsed throughout the years and
now lay upon the mounds further camouflaging the rusting
metal relics.

Unless you were aware that the ancient cars were there
or unless you were deliberately searching for them you
would be more likely than not to simply pass by the
enormous mass, thinking it to be nothing more than
natural forest growth.

But the creatures who resided in the forest knew the
old cars were there, hidden by the impenetrable
underbrush. The hollowed out battered skeletal remains
had become the perfect nesting places for a varied
assortment of wildlife. This automotive condominium of
sorts was so vast in magnitude that both predator and prey

could be found living somewhere within the ruins. A fox or coyote or feral mountain cat might have its den inside a '53 Cadillac Fleetwood, while only a few hundred feet away, a family of rabbits might reside in a '63 Ford Falcon.

This particular graveyard was located in the woods, just off of Route 51, on the winding range of hills between the community of Mountain Springs and the town of Franksville in Schuylkill County, Pennsylvania. Where there had once been a dirt and gravel access road nothing remained. Its original appearance was impossible to distinguish from the rest of the overgrown woodland.

If you were able to pinpoint what was once the road and then took it upon yourself to locate and unearth the metallic vestiges they would ascertain the most recent vehicle in the macabre collection, which was also the uppermost car on the stack, was a 1965 Mercury Monterey 4-door sedan. If you were then to investigate the history surrounding this particular vehicle in greater detail you would discover it had once been the property of one Anson Middleton of 1255 Race Street, Franksville, Pennsylvania.

Had you chosen to learn more about Mr. Middleton, you would have found that Middleton and his vehicle had been involved in a catastrophic automobile accident resulting in Mr. Middleton's death and the complete destruction of the Mercury. A similar story could be said about every single one of the cars on the massive pile of decomposing steel. Each car in the automotive graveyard had been involved in an accident that resulted in a fatality. And like Mr. Middleton's Cadillac; every vehicle had its own story to tell.

Who created this mountain of past sorrows remains a mystery as does the reason the collector might have chosen only to include those specific cars that had been involved in fatal accidents. Perhaps if someone were to question a few of the local old-timers they might be lucky enough to discover the answer. However, that would be unlikely, as few if any of those older folks who might still be alive would care to speak of the place.

Back in the 1960s the location was well known among the local bar patrons and had been discussed for hours on end until it eventually attained a status akin to legendary.

At one time, the barflies might have actually known the name of the person responsible for the automotive necropolis and might even have understood his reasons for creating it. But as with most legends the stories surrounding the site grew to the point where they became nothing more than tall tales.

But nowadays most of those same townsfolk were either dead or were simply so old that no one would bother to pay attention to what might be perceived as their wild ramblings. So as a result, over fifty years later, the mysterious final resting place was now forgotten along with most of its tragic stories.

But there are still a few your humble narrator has chosen to be recounted.

Anson Middleton's tale was one that was as riddled with clichés as it was tragic; the stuff of country-western tunes. Mr. Anson Middleton had once been a senior claims adjuster for the Competence Insurance Company of America. But on that fateful night when he had earned his place on the forest pile of the dead, Mr. Middleton was traveling in excess of 100 MPH while under the influence of a combination of alcohol and prescription drugs. His car left the roadway and slammed headlong into a bridge abutment, producing the predictable yet unpleasantly volatile and final results.

Now if you were to take the initiative to unearth every one of the vehicles you would learn that the very first car positioned at the bottom of the pile was a 1938 Packard Super Eight owned by Jeremiah T. Blakely, a well-to-do local doctor and resident of the nearby city of Yuengsville. His sad story was one of mechanical malfunction, which eventually led to extreme suffering and ultimately, death.

Jeremiah, his wife and two children had been enjoying a Sunday afternoon leisurely drive over the Wide-Top Mountain between the towns of Coalmansville and Horton when their brakes failed on the steep incline leading down into the little town. Their car quickly gained speed, and despite Jeremiah's best efforts to maintain control, the velocity soon became too excessive to navigate the automobile.

Since no guardrails were present during those early years, the car became airborne and flew over the hillside where it flipped end-for-end multiple times killing everyone inside, but sadly not instantly. One unknown fact about this tragedy was that Mr. Blakely was the last of his family to perish after being forced to spend the last few agonizing minutes of his life listening to the tortured suffering screams of his wife and family as one-by-one their cries faded as they succumbed to their excruciating injuries.

But perhaps the strangest and most haunting stories of all the tragic and horrible tales was the one concerning a young, abrasive, and arrogant teen named James "Duke" Wellington and a forty-something-year-old family man named Francis O'Halloran.

About halfway down the rusting pile of vehicles, circa 1952-1955, there lay the two corroded shells, which are the subject of this particular tale. The story of their arrival in the automotive graveyard is cloaked in conceit, wealth, influence, death, and eventual revenge.

James "Duke" Wellington was a sixteen-year-old foolhardy youth whose father happened to be a wealthy and politically well-connected local attorney. Jim got the nickname "Duke" because of the way his surname, Wellington, rhymed with the famous jazz pianist, composer and big band leader Duke Ellington. However, young Jim Wellington was unable to write music, play piano, or conduct a band. The Wellington family lived in an upper-class subdivision outside of Franksville.

In contrast, Francis O'Halloran was a forty-three-year-old father of four children, all of whom were under the age of sixteen. His eldest, Francis Junior, was in a class one year behind the infamous Duke Wellington. Young Francis had few if any encounters with Wellington but from observations he perceived the boy to be a bully. And like all bullies, Wellington traveled with a cadre of toadies, flunkies, and general hangers-on whose apparent sole purpose in life was to laugh at all of Wellington's juvenile pranks as well as his immature sense of humor.

Francis Sr. and his family lived in a small wood-framed lower-middle class row house in Ashton. They survived from paycheck to paycheck as did most of the people in his particular social strata. But he never complained and did all he could to support his family. He was a dedicated hard worker who was assigned to the job of second shift laborer at a local mirror manufacturing plant on the south side of Franksville.

One late winter night when the roads were treacherous and Francis was driving down the steep winding hill, heading home from his job, Duke was simultaneously traveling like the proverbial bat-out-of-hell up the hill from the opposite direction. His car was fishtailing wildly and traveling outside of his lane. Duke was accompanied by one of his friends, Nick Giamondi, both of them laughing hysterically at yet another of Duke's idiotic stunts. As fate would have it, the two cars met at the exact wrong time as the back end of Duke's '55 Corvette fishtailed into the oncoming lane and was struck by O'Halloran's 1953 Ford Country Squire Station Wagon. Normally such a collision would not have done much damage to the tank-like Ford, but at the last moment, in an ill-fated attempt to avoid the collision, O'Halloran turned his wheel too hard and lost control of the monstrous vehicle sliding across the highway, through the guardrails, down over the embankment, and finally slamming into a cluster of large trees, killing him instantly.

Duke's corvette was damaged somewhat in the back end and he suffered a fractured leg, while his friend Nick managed to escape with just a few cuts and lacerations. Police filed charges of vehicular homicide against young Wellington but his influential father helped him to get away just a fine, which his father   grudgingly paid. Likewise when the O'Halloran family tried to sue the Wellingtons in civil court, the results were just as unsuccessful.

Duke had escaped a jail sentence and a lawsuit. One might think such a close brush with the grim reaper might make him reflect; might even make him a bit humble, but it did not. In fact, in some people's opinions his arrogance seemed to have increased, as did the number and severity of the various twisted pranks he pulled on his classmates. For young Francis O'Halloran, Jr. the idea of watching the person who killed his father get off scot-free was often more than he could tolerate. But Francis was a small boy with few friends and his family did not travel in the same socio-economic circles as the Wellingtons, so the best he could hope for was to avoid any contact with Duke whatsoever. He feared that if Duke recognized him as the son of the woman who tried to sue him, he would suffer intolerable harassment at the hands of Duke and his army of cronies. So he kept a low profile and remained quiet, doing his best to operate below Duke's radar.

During the next two years before Duke's high school graduation many strange stories began to spread around the area about mysterious sightings at the very same curve where Francis O'Halloran lost his life that fateful night. Some people claimed to see a man standing near the side of the road as if looking and waiting for someone to drive by. One person said they stopped to offer the man a ride but when they opened the car door he was gone. Some people even went so far as to describe the man as looking like the late Francis O'Halloran, which of course started the rumor mill buzzing and before long all sorts of ghost stories began to permeate the region.

The O'Halloran family heard about the stories but did their best to ignore them as such tales only served to increase unhappy memories. Duke Wellington heard the stories as well, but his response was to simply scoff at them as nothing but utter nonsense. Yet during those years Duke had made a point of going far out of his way to avoid that particular stretch of highway. His corvette had been repaired shortly after the accident and although he still drove much faster than he should, he made a point to never travel that road again.

That was, until the night of his high school graduation when he was in a hurry to get home after a friend's party. Duke wanted to see what his father had bought him as a graduation gift. He had asked for a new corvette, as his current one was never quite the same since the accident; at least it never felt right to Duke again. And since his father always bought him everything he wanted, he was certain the new car was waiting for him at home.

Instead of taking his usual roundabout trip home he decided it made more sense to travel up the winding mountain and pass the site where the accident occurred.

Although he had been nervous about doing so, Duke talked himself into it, thinking about how as a high school graduate it was time for him to put his unfortunate past behind him and be a man.

As he approached the curve, which had caused him so much trouble two years earlier, Duke deliberately slowed his car so he would be certain to pass through safely. His first inclination was to drive past the site as quickly as possible, but slow and easy seemed the best choice on that dark and somewhat foggy night.

As he approached the bend Duke saw someone; a man, standing by the side of the road watching as if waiting. The man wore a denim blue work shirt and cotton workpants. His hair hung down over his eyes and at first Duke was not sure who he might be. Then the strange man lifted his head and stared directly at Duke who immediately recognized him as Francis O'Halloran, the man he had killed almost two years earlier. But the man no longer looked as he had back then.

Now the man's cheeks were sunken and his flesh was no more than sallow hide stretched tightly over bones. His eyes appeared huge and seemed to bug out of sunken black holes. His lips were mere lines pulled back over a mass of large exposed black and rotten teeth. The horrible creature opened his mouth and let out a roar that vibrated deep into Duke's skull, causing him to instinctively throw his hands up to protect his aching ears.

As he covered his ears he was just entering the curve and the vehicle started to veer off the highway. He quickly grabbed the wheel, overcompensating in the process. The car went into an uncontrollable spin before skidding off the highway and slamming into the same cluster of trees at the exact same spot where Francis O'Halloran lost his life two years earlier.

The police who arrived to clean up the mess could not help but notice the look of complete terror that remained on the face of the battered corpse of Duke Wellington. Since a few of them had been on the job a long time and had been the very same officers who had been called to the original O'Halloran/Wellington accident, they looked at each other with amazement; understanding the strange, unspoken coincidence. Once again the local rumor mill filled with stories of ghostly vengeance and how the spirit of Francis O'Halloran had come back from the grave to claim the life of the person who had taken his.

Since that night, sightings of the mysterious stranger stopped. No one ever saw anything unusual at the site of the crashes again, no matter how many stories were told. And they never would. This was because the two cars were now a mile or more deeper in the woods decaying in the middle of a stack of cars; and each of those cars had their own terrible stories to tell.

If you were to stop by the weed-infested pile of rusting metal late at night and if you were to sit quietly and listen with an ear for the uncommon, you might hear the painful cries of a young man and the maniacal laughter of revenge coming from his torturer as the two sounds blend to form a mournful howl in the darkness of night.

Double Yellow

*It must be I thought, one of the race's most persistent
and comforting hallucinations to trust that "it can't happen
here"—that one's own time and place is beyond cataclysm.*
—John Wyndahm, *The Day of the Triffids*

Wyatt drove robotically along the winding country two-
lane road. It was the same one he had traveled daily for
almost thirty years during his long commute to and from
work. Little had changed with that particular stretch of
highway during those many years save for the occasional
resurfacing project, followed by the repainting of the white
lines along the shoulders of the road as well as the solid
double yellow lines down the center.

This was Wyatt's first day returning to work as a
purchasing agent for a major corporation after being
absent the entire previous week, suffering with a
particularly nasty strain of some sort of flu bug that had
apparently been making its rounds. He had started feeling
poorly the previous Saturday morning and by evening he
was sicker than he had been in a very long time; exploding
from both ends as it were. Wyatt could imagine little that
might be worse as he had sat on the toilet with a bucket on
the floor in front of him just waiting for the next wave of
sickness to strike, which it often did simultaneously.

By Sunday night the worst of his illness was over but
he was feeling very weak, so Wyatt decided to take off
Monday to rest and recover before making any attempt at
returning to work. But when he discovered he felt no better
Tuesday morning he once again stayed home and slept
most of that day as well. Late Tuesday night he tried eating
some clear soup broth, which his wife had made for him,
hoping to feel well enough to return Wednesday. But as it
turned out, he didn't make it in Wednesday either. After

trying to do a few things around the house in a feeble attempt to get himself back to normal, he began to feel worse once again. So he took off Thursday and Friday as well.

He had decided it might be better to wait and start fresh on Monday. The weekend had gone fairly well and by Monday he was feeling about as good as he could be expected to feel after such an ordeal. Wyatt's wife suggested that what he really needed now was to get back into his daily routine and put the illness behind him. He was still a bit foggy in the brain but he guessed that was to be expected after being down for so long.

As he drove along the road in the early dawn darkness, Wyatt noticed the highway appeared somehow different than it had looked a week earlier. Something about it had changed. He could not quite determine what the difference was, however. At first he wondered if perhaps the state workers had resurfaced the two-lane while he was off, but he could see in the light from his high beams that the road had the same worn surface as previously. He always left for work before sunrise and arrived home after dark so he was accustomed to the way the road looked in his headlights. Yet still something definitely seemed different. He wondered what it might be. Then, he realized what it was: it was the lines.

That was it. Apparently someone must have repainted the traffic lines during his time away. The single white lines along the shoulders seemed much whiter and the solid double yellow lines down the center glowed with a sort of phosphorescence the likes of which Wyatt had not noticed before.

He wondered why anyone would have bothered to repaint the markings on a road that was in such dire need of resurfacing. It made no fiscal sense and the contrast between the lines and the worn highway surface was almost disturbing. Then Wyatt looked more closely at the lines and suspected he might have been incorrect and perhaps they had not been repainted after all. Yet the lines still did seem to stand out from the rest of the roadway for some unexplainable reason.

Maybe it was the result of some strange convergence of atmospheric conditions; the darkness of the predawn; the position of the moon and stars combined with the absence of clouds. Perhaps he was viewing the lines through a magnifying morning mist. Who knew? For whatever reason, the lines seemed to glow with an incredible iridescence. Then Wyatt noticed something else about the lines that he could not begin to explain—they suddenly made him feel very uncomfortable.

For the first time in all of his years of traveling along the same road, Wyatt felt as if he was a prisoner being held captive by the lines. Although he understood such a thought was illogical as well as completely irrational he couldn't seem to shake the sensation, which was beginning to feel almost claustrophobic. Perhaps he was still feeling the effects of his illness of the previous week and it was playing tricks with his mind. But whatever the reason, the feeling was extremely intense.

In his heart, Wyatt understood the lines were there for public safety. In fact, both sets of lines were accompanied by rumble strip grooves cut in the highway beneath them so if a driver started to doze at the wheel and his car began to cross the lines he would be awakened by the sound and feel of his tires on the grooves and it might prevent him from hurting himself or others. Like the lines themselves, the rumble strips were there to protect motorists and to help enforce traffic control regulations.

"Control," Wyatt thought suddenly. Yes, wasn't that their real purpose? Wasn't that the true reason for the lines? To control the flow of traffic? To control the actions of the motorists? Or perhaps their purpose was much more sinister than that.

He began to question if just maybe the double yellow lines were just one more method the government might be using to manipulate him and his fellow motorists; to force them to adhere to yet another ridiculous bureaucratic regulation. Control simply for the sake of control.

"What if there were no lines?" he thought to himself. Then he wondered if he suddenly found himself on a blank roadway with no lines in sight, would he stupidly veer over into the opposite lane, into the path of oncoming traffic and be involved in a collision? Or would he go off the roadway to the right and smash into a tree or maybe drive over an embankment? He was quite certain he would not. The very thought was ridiculous. But then again, if it were really dark, foggy, raining, or snowing heavily, without the benefit of the brightly painted lines he might inadvertently do just that.

So he reluctantly accepted that the true purpose for the lines was nothing sinister, but that they were simply there for his own welfare. In fact, he was beginning to question the rationale of his own earlier thoughts and was wondering why he was becoming so foolishly fixated on something as mundane and trivial as double yellow highway lines in the first place. The lines kept him driving safely on his side of the road the oncoming traffic on their side. But then Wyatt began to wonder if the lines really did do their required job of keeping people on their respective sides of the roadway after all.

Now Wyatt's heart seemed to skip a beat when he realized the naivety of his last series of thoughts. The lines were just that; simply painted markings. They had no mystic or magical powers. In fact, they were not a real barrier in any true sense of the word. Even with the warning rumble strips cut into the road beneath the lines, they could do nothing to prevent someone from crossing over and slamming headlong into his car. Wyatt had read countless newspaper stories of drivers who had either passed out or had heart attacks while driving, then crossed the double yellow lines, crashing into the oncoming vehicles.

And how many accounts had he read of drunk drivers doing the same thing? Wyatt realized as if for the first time, the lines did absolutely nothing to protect him from the potential madness of the drivers in the oncoming lane. He was starting to realize what a game of Russian roulette it was to simply drive down the highway on a daily basis. Any driver he might encounter at any moment could be the bullet; the one destined to cross the lines, crash into him and take him out.

Then as if horribly on cue, a set of overly bright headlights appeared in the distance coming toward Wyatt in the opposite lane. At least he hoped the lights were still in the opposite lane. From his distance he couldn't tell for certain. The lights could just as easily have been in his own lane, heading straight for him. This could be it, he thought; the one potential fatality fate had chosen to attach his name to. Wyatt broke out in a cold sweat, thinking about how the only thing standing between him, the oncoming car, and imminent death was a double yellow line painted on the road surface. His hands began to tremble as the headlights got closer.

He imagined a deadly scenario in which the driver of the oncoming car might have been depressed over some personal tragedy; perhaps an unfaithful wife or girlfriend or perhaps the upsetting death of a loved one. If the driver were despondent enough, he might very easily decide to drive insanely into Wyatt's car in a sudden suicidal impulse. If that were to happen there would be no way Wyatt could get out of the vehicle's path in time.

As the car got closer Wyatt saw it was still on its proper side of the road, but he didn't feel in any way assured it would stay there. When the car got even closer Wyatt's hands became wet with sweat and he could feel rivulets of perspiration trickling down the center of his back. Then a moment later it was over. The car had passed by and its taillights were a mere shrinking memory in his rearview mirror.

Wyatt began to wonder what he would have done if the person in the other car actually had come over into his lane. He looked over to the right of the roadway and saw about a two feet wide shoulder, which dropped off into a deep culvert for water drainage. A few feet beyond that was a row of telephone poles. There was absolutely nowhere for him to safely go in that direction.

Then he looked to his left, thinking that if a car came most of the way over into his lane he might be able to squeeze through on that side, but he saw another short shoulder and an even steeper drop off, behind which was a slight embankment thick with trees. Perhaps if he made it to the culvert on that side his car might be totaled, but at least he had a chance of surviving. Then the strange stream of thoughts once again raced through his mind; he truly was trapped between the lines on the highway like a prisoner with no means of escape.

"What in the hell is wrong with me?" Wyatt asked aloud, suddenly realizing the potential problems that would be brought on by implications the unfortunate series of emotions he had just experienced. "Wyatt, you idiot. You have got to get a grip."

He had no idea what was going on with his head or why the weird luminescent double-yellow lines had brought on such feelings of discomfort, if not almost crippling terror. But whatever it might have been he had to make it stop and quickly. Wyatt still had to drive an hour to work each way every day and unless he could find some method to suppress the horrified emotional state he suddenly found himself in, he would not be able to return to his job. And Wyatt knew that no job meant no money.

For a moment he seriously considered turning around and heading home, realizing perhaps he was not as well as he originally assumed. "Maybe if I stay home for another day or two things will work themselves out and then I'll be back to normal." He had only traveled about ten of his fifty minute commute so he still had the majority of his trip ahead of him. But he knew the idea of turning around was impractical. What would he say to his wife? The terror he felt deep in the pit of his stomach was irrational, he was certain. He knew he felt fine physically, but it was his brain that for some reason seemed to be giving him all the trouble; that and those strange glowing double yellow lines.

As he cleared the top of a hill Wyatt could see the interstate out in the distance, not more than three or four miles away. He realized if he could make it to that major four-lane roadway with its guardrails and large grass-planted median strips separating the oncoming lanes he would be fine.

It can't be more than five minutes away. Wyatt thought. If I can just avoid other cars for the next few miles, I will be home safe. That was when he saw a new set of headlights in the distance coming toward him.

"Oh my God, no!" Wyatt said. "Not another one." Once again he immediately broke out in an icy sweat. First his upper lip and forehead began to lightly bead with moisture.

The other car was getting closer now, its headlights growing in size. Wyatt was certain that the car was slightly veering over toward his side of the road.

The beads of sweat had now formed rivulets running down his face as well as the center of his back. Wyatt could feel his heart start to beat faster in his chest. He involuntarily gripped the steering wheel tighter although his palms were so wet he could barely maintain his hold.

Then he saw the car was definitely crossing over into his lane; Wyatt was certain of it. He could hear the steady thumping in his brain as his blood pulsed rapidly though his body. It grew louder by the second, sounding like the foot pedal of a heavy-metal drummer, high on some illegal substance, manically slamming against a bass drum.

Wyatt felt a sudden pressure in the middle of his chest as if someone twice his size had just sat on top of him, trying to crush the very life out of him. He felt a sharp pain coursing down his left arm. The world around him started to fade and grow darker. He could scarcely hear the thudding of the rumble strips over the pounding of his heart. The last thing Wyatt saw were the headlights of the suicidal maniac's oncoming car heading straight for him.

***

"Damn shame," the township patrolman said to the state trooper in frustration.

"What do you suppose happened?" The trooper inquired.

The patrolman explained, pointing to the woman standing outside of a minivan, which was halfway off the opposite side of the highway and wedged down in the culvert.

"That woman over there said she was on her way to town to get a coffee before taking her two kids to daycare. The two kids are OK as well, thanks to their car seats. Anyway, she said she was driving along when suddenly that car crossed the double yellow lines into her lane, heading right for her. Luckily, at the last minute she managed to turn sharply to her left and just miss getting hit. The driver of that sedan went off the road, down into the culvert, rolled over once, and slammed into a tree. It appears the driver was killed instantly."

The trooper asked, "So what are you thinking? Heart attack?"

"Most likely," the patrolman replied. "He is the right age, overweight, and his skin appears to be dusky in color, likely from lack of oxygen."

"Well," the trooper replied. "I suppose that lady and her two kids are lucky she was able to get out of the way at the last minute. Otherwise we would have a real mess to clean up. This is bad enough."

The patrolman said, "Yeah. Every time something like this happens I realize just how vulnerable we are, when the only thing separating us from disaster is a painted double-yellow line."

"I agree." The trooper replied. "Kind of makes you not want leave home in the morning."

Twick Oa Tweet

Conscience is no more than the dead speaking to us.
—Jim Carroll

Ghosts crowd the young child's fragile eggshell mind.
—Jim Morrison

Not a single one of the residents of the quiet upscale subdivision of Wellington Estates understood why it was that their reclusive neighbor, William Elverson, divorced, age forty-eight, hated Halloween with such a passion. And because of Elverson's less than outgoing demeanor no one ever managed to feel close enough to the man to ask him why that might be. Or perhaps they simply didn't care enough to try to discover the answer. But it was nonetheless obvious to everyone in the neighborhood that Elverson detested the holiday.

Every year, the entire subdivision went all out to make the holiday a festive event with elaborate house decorations including lights, props, and even a few animatronic displays. Some lawns were adorned with large cheerful-looking inflatable cartoon-like decorations. Others took a more sinister approach having chosen to transform their frontage into frightening graveyard scenes. Ghosts, ghouls, and goblins abounded, as did various incarnations of vampires, werewolves, zombies, famous Hollywood slashers and every monster imaginable.

A few of the residents even went to the next level of Halloween enthusiasm and converted their large two and three-car garages into makeshift haunted houses, complete with billowing gray fog and movie quality scenery with frighteningly realistic makeup and stereo sound effects. As a result on Halloween night literally hundreds of revelers walked through the development with their children, turning the entire neighborhood into one big Halloween party. As the word spread, families from other neighborhoods made the pilgrimage to see what new ideas the folks managed to come up with.

But not William; he would never do a single thing to participate in the annual festivities. In fact, most people couldn't help but notice how every year on the evening of October thirty-first, when every other house in the neighborhood was aglow with Halloween decorations, William's house was cast into darkness and his car was nowhere to be found. Ironically, in many ways the lack of decoration and the solitary darkness surrounding his home on Halloween night often made it seem more frightening and more sinister than even the most elaborately decorated property.

William's absence likewise did not go unnoticed by the various kids of the neighborhood, especially those who were of the more malicious ilk. These creatively nefarious juveniles took the letter of the law when it came to "Trick or Treat" and felt that Elverson's obvious absence and snubbing of their favorite holiday granted them carte blanche to play whatever pranks they could imagine and even commit minor acts of vandalism on the man's property.

These hoodlums rationalized that if William had chosen not to be home on Halloween night to offer them treats then it was their right and perhaps even their duty to play any tricks on the man they deemed appropriate. As a result, Every November first William awoke to find the trees in his front yard draped with long, flowing streamers of toilet paper. On more than one occasion William had returned to his property Halloween night to find his doorbell had been taped down in the ringing position and the window to his storm door had been coated with soap-streaked vulgarities obviously added by some of the more daring of the neighborhood kids.

And on one unfortunate occasion, the legendary flaming bag of poo had been set afire, fortunately on his concrete walkway so no real damage could be done to his home. That particular incident ended up being more symbolic than effective and in reality was an exercise in futility, since William never was home to rush from the house to stomp out the fire, completing the gag.

If the people of the neighborhood would have taken the time to get to know William better, they might have possibly had a better understanding or at least an appreciation for his avoidance of the holiday. They would also know why he had been avoiding the holiday every year since he was just a child. But then again, William Elverson was not the type of person who cared enough to know or associate with any of his neighbors. He was a quiet, reclusive, and antisocial man who tended to keep to himself. Even the neighbors living right next door to William knew very little about him.

Elverson's lack of congeniality was largely the result of his melancholy disposition. Even before his divorce, he and his wife had been less than sociable, but since the split, he had become more of a loner and a recluse. This made him seem an oddball of the neighborhood.

This aspect of his personality however, had little to do with his displeasure with the Halloween season. That particular dislike was the result of an event that was much more horrifying and completely life changing. William had only been eight years old when an unspeakable tragedy had occurred, altering his personality forever.

William, who was known back then as Billy, and his best friend, Jimmy Jenson, had been trick or treating in their neighborhood on that fateful Halloween night forty years earlier. The two young boys had been friends forever, so it seemed, and every year they anxiously awaited the arrival of Halloween, which had been one of their favorite holidays.

The two boys enjoyed dressing in costumes and pretending to be someone or something they were not, as all kids did. They also loved and anticipated filling their sacks with candy and treats. Although they had participated in the trick or treat ritual for as long as they both could remember, that particular Halloween night was a very special time for both of them.

It was the first year the boys' parents had consented to allow them to go from house to house unescorted. In the past, one or both of their parents had always gone along with them, waiting by the curb not only to protect them from any of the larger kids who might want to steal their treats but as a warning to the homeowners that they would be checking their boys' treat bags and the candies before either of them would be allowed to eat any of it. There had been reports in the newspapers over the previous years about treat tampering, as well as urban legends of razorblades in apples and laxatives injected into chocolates and other such horrible acts. The presence of the parents was to serve as a deterrent to any such abhorrent behavior.

The lack of parental accompaniment that year was a significant turning point in both of the boys' young lives as it indicated they were no longer considered little kids but were now big boys; old enough to trick or treat on their own. This was especially important to Jimmy, who had been burdened with a very noticeable speech impediment—what many of the neighborhood children referred to as "baby talk." He said his Ls and Rs like Ws as in "Maawy had a wittle wamb," sounding a lot like the cartoon character Elmer Fudd. He had been going to special speech classes at the elementary school to try to break him of the speech defect, but progress was slow going. Billy didn't mind the way Jimmy talked because Jimmy was his best friend.

On that particular Halloween night, young Billy was dressed in a homemade pirate costume and Jimmy wore cowboy getup, complete with red felt hat and neckerchief. Billy had thought Jimmy's costume was a bit too young looking for him and did nothing to help him shed the baby image, which haunted him because of his speech. But they were best friends and as far as Billy was concerned, if that was what Jimmy wanted to wear then so be it.

The night had been a very successful one for the both of them as they had been making a good haul and their candy sacks were bulging with treats. Billy was tired and wanted to go home, but Jimmy was excited and wanted to try one more house before calling it a night. He pointed down the street, indicating he had found his final target for the night.

The house that Jimmy had chosen was the last house at the end of a street, which dead-ended at a vacant lot. Beyond the lot lay the edge of a local forest, cast in shadow beyond the glow of the streetlights.

Billy was reluctant to approach the house because it appeared to be a ramshackled wreck in such dire disrepair; he doubted anyone actually lived there any longer. They did notice, however, there was an inviting light glowing on the paint-chipped ceiling of the dilapidated front porch, which was a signal all kids immediately recognized as the universal beacon of welcome for young costumed children on that most mysterious of nights.

The two boys approached the front stairs apprehensively, Jimmy taking the lead and Billy following a few cautious steps behind him. Billy suggested, "Jimmy. I think we should skip this place . . . it sort of gives me the creeps. Something just don't feel right about it."

"Aw, c'mon," Jimmy insisted. "Stop bein such a baby, Biwwy. Theao ain't nothin wong with dis pwace. Pwobably some owd guy wivves here oa somethin wike dat." Billy had been so accustomed to hearing Jimmy speak with his baby-like quality, that he had understood every single word the boy had said, even though he doubted others would have.

Ignoring Billy's protests, Jimmy boldly walked up to the rickety front door and knocked hard on its surface several times. The door seemed to rattle in its frame and the broken front window tinkled from the vibration as if threatening to fall out and come crashing onto the porch. When he didn't get a reply, Jimmy knocked yet again, harder.

Eventually, a gruff-sounding voice called out, "What d'ya want?" The tonal quality of the voice, a man's voice and a sinister sound that seemed to lie just beneath the spoken words, made Billy quake with fear. The voice sounded very wrong and Billy got a strange sensation in the pit of his stomach. But Jimmy was not intimidated in any way by the strange tone and simply replied, "Twick oa tweet, Mista."

For a moment, nothing happened. Billy pleaded with Jimmy to leave the place and head home. He even considered turning and running away himself, but his feet felt heavy like they sometimes did in bad dreams. Then, before he could do or say anything several things occurred in a matter of just a few seconds. Billy saw these horrifying things played out as if watching a movie in slow motion. Suddenly the overhead porch light switched out, plunging the boys into total darkness. Before their eyes could completely adjust to the sudden blackness, and before they could even consider turning and running, the front door burst open inward with a rattling bang, the already cracked glass shattering and falling in a tinkling rain of shards somewhere inside the house.

As his eyes came into focus, Billy saw two grimy, scab-covered hands reaching out from the darkness of the house. They grabbed Jimmy's arms and pulled the now screaming child inside. For a moment, Billy stood in terror, mouth agape, unable to comprehend what he should do next. It was so much like a bad dream as he stood frozen with fear.

Then, suddenly reacting, not thinking, Billy did what any young defenseless boy would likely do in a similar situation. He turned screaming, dropping his cache of candy to the ground, and ran home in terror. The street was dark and deserted so there was no one around to hear his cries for help. He ran madly, occasionally venturing a glance behind him assuming some horrible denizen of the night was bearing down upon him. As he ran toward his house, the streetlights glistened like stars through his tear-filled eyes.

When he finally arrived home, Billy was confused and uncertain about what to do next. He wanted to scream for his mother and father but he felt ashamed of the tears flowing down his face. He wanted to be alone, just for a little while to figure out how he should handle everything. He was terribly worried about Jimmy but was mixed up and unsure of what to think. He didn't want his family to see him crying like a baby, so he bypassed his brothers and sisters and hurried directly up to his bedroom where he crawled into his bed, pulled the covers over his head, and sobbed uncontrollably.

After a few minutes, his mother came into his room and asked Billy what was wrong. He tried to hold back his emotions but instantly broke down. Tearfully, he recounted the events with as much detail as his terrified young mind would allow. His mother immediately called the local police then called Jimmy's parents. Within ten minutes, both had arrived at the Elverson home, and with Billy's guidance the group found the house where Billy said Jimmy had been abducted. Their spilled sacks of candy still covered the front porch, but Billy was no longer hungry for candy and didn't ever want to think of Halloween treats again.

The police eventually discovered the house was a vacant property but had not actually been abandoned. Its owner had recently passed away after years of being aged and infirm. That explained the dilapidated condition of the property. However, the electricity had not yet been disconnected. Upon examining the house that night the police found it was unoccupied, although they discovered the back door lock was broken, obviously the route the perpetrator had used to gain entrance and likely the same door he had used to make his escape. It was located on the forest side of the house so the vagrant was able to enter unseen. Other than the spilled bag of candy they found no trace of Jimmy.

Billy overheard one police officer tell his mother, "If your boy would have just told you sooner, maybe we could have gotten here in time to help Jimmy. But too much time has been allowed to pass. And now to be honest, I'm afraid it just doesn't look very good." Billy was stricken with guilt and grief at the thought that his inaction was likely responsible for whatever might have happened to his best friend. But Billy knew he was just a little kid, he wasn't supposed to know what to do in such a situation. Heck, stuff like that wasn't supposed to happen to little kids. But this knowledge didn't help ease his young conscience.

After several weeks of futile searching, a hunter inadvertently came upon the boy's decomposed remains buried in a shallow grave in a nearby forest, still dressed in his Halloween cowboy costume; filthy with coagulated blood, rotting flesh and dirt. The young boy's corpse had been partially consumed by rats, birds, insects, and a variety of other small forest creatures.

The medical examiner was able to determine that prior to his death; young Jimmy had been tortured and sexually assaulted. Eventually he mercifully succumbed to his injuries. Then even more than previously, young Billy found himself wracked with guilt, hearing the police officer's comments about him echoing in his mind over and over again. "If your boy would have just told you sooner . . . would have just told you sooner . . . told you sooner . . . sooner."

From that day on, Billy never went out trick or treating on Halloween night again and each year stayed locked in his room, in bed with the covers drawn tightly over his head until the night was over. And as he hid in terror, in his mind Billy relived the horrible events of the night he lost his best friend.

Sometimes on the more disturbing Halloween nights, Billy believed he could hear tapping at his window and imagined he also heard a small voice in the wind saying "Biwwy . . . Biwwwy . . ." He imagined the small skeletal hands of his long dead friend scratching on the windowsill, trying his best to find a way inside; to get to Billy.

As an adult, each year for past forty years, William Elverson did everything in his power to avoid Halloween. When the rest of his neighborhood was busy greeting the throng of costumed children, William would instead leave his house for the evening returning only after the 9:00 pm curfew; it was the only way he could make sure no children would come ringing his doorbell. He could not bear the thought of seeing them; he was filled with the irrational belief that one fateful day his long-dead friend might be hiding somewhere among them, waiting for his chance to get back at Billy for his unforgivable act of cowardice.

This Halloween night it had been raining heavily and although it was only eight-thirty, William was certain there would be no more kids about, so he decided to break tradition and head back to his house a bit earlier than normal. As he suspected, his street appeared to be deserted. He pulled his car into his garage and quickly closed the door, keeping all of the lights turned out.

William sat in his family room at the rear lower level of his, home watching TV, out of site of the street. As far as anyone outside was concerned, his house appeared to be uninhabited, which was just fine with William.

After a few minutes, as he sat and watched television with the sound turned way down, William heard a light knocking at his front door. He tried to ignore it, until he heard it again, but louder. And then he heard the knocking once again even more forcefully. William became irritated. He had his lights turned off and there was no reason for anyone to be knocking on his door. He had just about had enough of the neighborhood and the damned kids who lived there. Who did they think they were? Didn't he have a right to his own privacy?

William decided he would go upstairs to the front door and give the apparently impudent child a stern lecture about his inappropriate behavior. He approached the front door and looked out through the peephole but could not see anyone at first. Then straining to look downward, he saw what appeared to be the top of a hat; a red felt cowboy hat of a variety he had not seen since his childhood. The hat appeared to be caked with dirt and grime.

William Elverson stood silently for a moment, a sick sinking feeling forming in the pit of his stomach. Cold droplets of sweat began to bead on the back of his neck quickly trickling along his flesh as an icy chill crept down his spine. He suddenly no longer felt like lecturing anyone and he heard himself asking uncertainly though the door, "What d'ya want?"

He immediately realized how frighteningly similar his now older croaking voice sounded to that horrible murder's he had heard coming from behind the door of the abandoned house on that Halloween night, so many years ago.

"Twick oa tweet, Mista," The voice said from the front porch with a baby talk quality William immediately recognized, and he was certain what awaited him on the other side of the door. He realized after so many years of avoidance, fate had finally caught up with him. He had tried to run for forty years but he could run no longer. It was time for him to face his destiny and if necessary to beg for forgiveness. His hands trembled with terror as they tried to grip the doorknob while wet with sweat.

William slowly opened the front door and looked upon the rotting remains of his once best friend, Jimmy Jensen, standing in his filthy shredded cowboy costume, his skeletal hand extended as if in anticipation of a treat. William looked into the creature's black-ringed dead eyes and imagined he saw the flesh sliding from the child's rotting face, as worms squirmed just below the surface of his skin, actively boring holes through the decaying flesh. In his mind he could smell the deep earthen odor from the undead child's former shallow forest grave.

The hideous creature again looked up at William and with a gap-toothed grin and said, "Twick oa tweet." The incredible shock of this hideous ghost from his past was too much for William to bear, as he collapsed to the floor in a heap, his heart stopping instantly dead in his chest from the inconceivable horror of the blasphemous specter before him.

Later, after the ambulance had removed William's still cooling body and the police were asking their questions, the young boy, named Sammy Wilkins, still dressed in his amazingly realistic zombie cowboy costume cried openly, cradled in his father's arms. The boy was confused, not knowing what had happened to the strange man in the house who had come to the door, and feeling like he might have done something to cause it to happen. His father assured him it was not his fault and that the man was probably sick.

Both Sammy and his father knew his Halloween costume was scary. After all, they had both worked very hard for several weeks to make it so. Sammy's father was a big Halloween enthusiast and amateur make-up artist, who enjoyed making costumes as terrifying and realistic as possible. However, he never thought that one of his costumes could have been realistic enough to have the potential to cause someone to die from fright. But apparently, he had been tragically wrong.

The Path

No one saves us but ourselves. No one can and no one may. We ourselves must walk the path.
—Buddha

The hot, stagnant space was almost black as Winston slowly regained consciousness. The only available light came from a single candle burning at the far end of the blackened cave. He instantly knew by the stinking hot and humid feel and the vile, recognizable odor that he was in a cave. Then again, each time Winston was forced to endure what he knew was coming it was always in one cave or another. A familiar sulfurous, noxious stench permeated the air, along with the coppery scent he recognized all too well as the reek of coagulating blood.

As he gradually awoke each of his nerve endings began sending rapid-fire messages to his sensory receptors and he started to feel the pain grow from an unpleasant discomfort to overwhelming agony. When he finally regained awareness Winston screamed with a painful howl as the tendrils of fiery hell shot up and down his body like a relentless storm of white-hot electric anguish. It was always this way, again and again, time after time, seemingly without end. He had no idea for how long or how many times he had been forced to endure similar suffering; he had lost count a long, long time ago.

Winston couldn't understand the physics of how he was made to feel the horrible effects of the relentless torment; yet the pain was nevertheless always present and very real. He was aware that he was dead and had been for what seemed to him like an eternity. He understood he was now nothing more than a spirit, a tortured soul. He was no longer corporal and as such—had no flesh, no bones, no no brain, no physical apparatuses whatsoever—yet he was somehow forced to constantly endure the sensation of pain which felt as agonizingly real to him as if he were still a living, breathing, physical human being. Winston comprehended that for some unexplainable reason he had been plunged into his own personal version of Hell, which apparently was to be his fate for time without end. He couldn't imagine what he had ever done in his life to deserve such constant torment, but it must have been more severe than he realized. Why else would he have been forced to tolerate an existence of such never ending suffering?

Tears flowed freely down his haggard face and when he tried to move he realized that, as was typical, he had been tightly secured and was incapable of any motion. Near the back of the coal-black cave Winston saw another candle slowly come to life; then another and another. These unbearable sessions always progressed in the same manner. Winston would awaken to find himself cast in total darkness and suffering with intolerable misery. Then slowly the candles would begin to light one by one until the room was awash with light. When all the candles were ablaze Winston would once again see for himself what manor of torture had been put upon him as well as what type of heinous demon was assigned the responsibility of inflicting his pain.

Once that had been revealed, the fire in his non-existent body would steadily grow to a level even more unbearable, if such a thing were possible, spurred on by the addition of this visually terrifying aspect of his torture. Eventually he would succumb to his pain and fall back into the blessed blackness. When his time in whatever particular room of torment was over he would find himself outside of the cave on what he thought of as the Path. Then he would once again be required to walk along the Path to the next available room, where, once inside, a new and even more horrifying form of torture awaited him. Oh yes, Winston had no doubt this was Hell.

As more of the candles sprang to life the room became ablaze with their glow and in his immobile state, Winston could only see directly in front of him. Against the far wall of the cave was a large area with an irregularly-shaped reflective stone embedded inside. At first Winston could not see well, but after a few moments of blinking away his blurring tears he saw his own reflection—and then wished he hadn't.

Earlier, Winston had felt some pain in his forehead, but had not known, nor could he imagine the cause, but now he suddenly understood the horrid truth. Winston could see in the reflective stone there was some type of rusted barbed wire wrapped in a circle around his head and its sharp spines had dug deep furrows into the flesh. Dried blood tracks covered his face. He looked strangely like pictures he had seen of Christ with his crown of thorns. But there was no Jesus Christ in this unholy place. Then he noticed something previously inconceivable happening above the encircling barbed crown.

He had to strain to look more closely to make sure he was not imagining what he was seeing. He could not believe the site before him. The entire top of his skull had been removed and his brain sat completely exposed. As if that fact alone was not disturbing enough, he realized that dozens of thin rusted metal pins or rods of some sort were scattered about and imbedded deep into his unprotected brain. And although the horrifying sight repulsed him beyond his worst imaginings, strangely he could not feel any pain in his skull, other than the superficial pain he originally felt from the barbed wire. What he did feel however, was a fiery misery in his arms.

Winston followed his gaze in the reflective stone down along his body and saw he had been placed in a large wooden-framed chair, curiously resembling the electric chairs used in the early days of Earth's death penalty executions. The wood was thick and heavy and deliberately uncomfortable. Winston could tell by the pain he was starting to feel in his buttocks that something had likely been placed on the seat to increase his level of discomfort; they always used something that felt like broken glass, metal shards, razor wire, or hot coals, but for some blessed reason he was not quite able to feel it as intently as believed he should have. And that was fine with him because the pain he already felt in his arms was unbearable enough.

As he continued to try to determine the level his unfortunate situation, Winston saw that he was naked, which also was not a surprise, as he had been naked since arriving in this horrible place so long ago. In fact, it seemed like everyone in Hell was naked. But there was no sexual reason for the nudity. The obvious purpose for the exposure was to make access easier for the armies of pain inflicting demons.

Then in the foggy mirror-stone Winston saw why his arms had been hurting him so badly. Oh my God, no! he thought as he bellowed out yet another blood curdling scream. In the matter of a second, time seemed to stop as Winston took in the extent of what the vile demon of this particular torture chamber had done to him.

Both of his wrists were secured to the top of the heavy arms of the chair buy two large rusted spikes driven down through them, essentially crucifying him to the arms of the chair. He thought again about his wire crown, about Jesus Christ and the blasphemy portrayed in Winston's own painful crucifixion. In the mirror he could see that his fingers, which were curled around the front of the arms, had been relieved of all of their flesh and most of the musculature, leaving only skeletal remains, which he was strangely still able to move although doing so only caused him increased pain.

As if that was not bad enough, he could see that the area behind his wrists and up to the tops of his forearms had suffered the worst of the damage. Strips of bloody flesh perhaps a half inch wide had been peeled back the length of his arms and curled up into rolls that were pierced and held together with long tarnished pins.

Each forearm had ten or more of these crimson coils of flayed flesh and Winston could see his own exposed red glistening muscles dripping with blood reflecting in the light. To Winston, it didn't matter that what he was seeing was not physical because the agony he felt most certainly was.

He prayed for this particular session to soon be over long before the real pain began, yet he knew his prayers would go unanswered as they always did. Hell was no place for prayer. Winston also understood, once his time in this particular torture chamber was over there would be another, even more unbearable period of pain waiting somewhere further up the Path.

"How you like me work? Good job, no?" Winston heard an ominous guttural voice, not possibly human in origin, say from behind him. Like most of the hideous beings that were responsible for inflicting pain, this one was no doubt another moronic monosyllabic beast whose sole purpose for existence was to exact untold levels of agony. Winston slowly pulled his eyes away from his throbbing arms and looked into the reflective stone to see an incredibly heinous looking demon standing behind him. This abomination stood over seven feet tall and was rail thin but sinewy with ropy muscles. Its fingers were long and bony and had great yellowed talons. Like the rest of the creatures Winston had previously encountered, its face was pig-like in appearance with a pushed up snout and a large slobbery mouth from which long fangs jutted both upward and downward. Its cat-shaped eyes bugged from the sunken sockets of its skull and it had two long ram horns curling back from its forehead continuing over top of a long mane of greasy black hair. It stank like a filthy barnyard animal and its grayish flesh, sporadically adorned with long, rat-like hairs, glistened with sweat adding to its already obnoxious stench.

The horrifying thing grinned sheepishly at Winston in the reflection and slowly lifted its right clawed hand upward toward the area atop Winston's head where his vulnerable brain had been stippled with so many pins.

"Humm." The horrid creature said, "It have too many pins. You don't feel 'nuff ouches." With that, the creature began to meticulously extract one pin after another from Winston's brain. With each pull of a pin the level of pain intensified until it reached its crescendo and Winston once again found himself blessedly, albeit temporarily unconscious.

***

When he started to regain awareness again, Winston suddenly recalled the details of what he had just been through and reflexively grabbed for his head and arms, certain he would find them still ripped and exposed. But they were not. He was whole once again, still naked, outside of the room where he had just endured one of the worst sessions to date. He was also momentarily free of pain and he knew he would have to enjoy whatever small amount of blessed relief he might have. It wouldn't last long, although it seemed time, at least as Winston understood time, was without meaning in this place.

Long ago, a demon in one of his many intervals of torment had mentioned to him that in Hell, a thousand years of pain could take place while only a few seconds passed in terms of earth time. Likewise just a few moments in Hell might be a century on the other side. Although the creature was not intelligent enough to articulate what he wanted to explain, Winston was able to take the beast's grunts and half sentences and turn them into what he thought might be a cohesive representation of the concept. He deduced that in Hell, the relationship of time was not linear; neither did it always go forward. Sometimes time stood still and sometimes it might even move backward depending on the particular need.

As Winston sat peacefully on the Path he knew exactly what he had to do next; he knew the routine. He was never allowed to sit for very long. He would have to eventually get up and begin walking to whatever door he was supposed to find next. Failure to do so would mean more severe repercussions in the next room. He also knew he could not go backwards and would not even consider attempting to do so. He had made that mistake once shortly after his arrival and discovered he was forced to go through every single agonizing second of every torture he had previously encountered all over again; from the beginning. That was only after five or six sessions. Now with literally thousands of periods of torture behind him he didn't want to even look behind him let alone try to go backward.

He stood up and looked out in the distance. Although he could only see for about fifty or sixty feet ahead of him in the dimly lit cavern he instinctively knew that the Path was endless. Spaced irregularly along both sides of the Path were doors made of large, heavy wooden planks bolted together with huge rusted iron hinges. The doors had no windows and were mounted into the stone cavern walls providing the only access into or out of each chamber. Winston learned shortly after his arrival that the rules of Hell were simple; walk forward on the Path and look for the next open door.

As he slowly made his way along the Path, Winston heard screaming of other unfortunate souls from behind those doors that were closed. The large main cavern was ceaselessly resonant with the unending shrieks of the damned. But despite the screams of the multitudes, Winston never met anyone else either in Hell or on the Path. That was another apparent rule of Hell; he was always alone except for those times of immeasurable suffering when he was in the capable hands of a vile demon.

Next to each of the doors hung a candelabrum formed from a real once living human hand, their withered gray fingers pointing upward as if reaching to catch some unknown object falling from a nonexistent sky. Melted fast to the cupped palm of each hand was a thick blood red candle; the hot wax dripping down forming puddles in the palm before spilling over and sliding along its shriveled forearm. The candles never seemed to burn down.

Not long after his arrival in Hell, Winston had been naturally curious and reached out to touch one of the hideous appendages, thinking them cast from stone because of their veined appearance, and was frighteningly greeted with the icy chill of dead, rotting human flesh. Then the hand had actually moved, ever so slightly; just enough to send chills down Winston's spine and to teach him one of his first of many lessons. It seemed to him as if almost every single minute in the horrible place he was learning something new whether he wanted to or not, and each new lesson was more horrifying than the last.

Winston kept the gruesome sconces in his peripheral vision as he slowly walked along the Path, among the howls of the countless damned, searching for the next open door; which he unfortunately saw up ahead. He understood the opening was meant for him and as such, was to be his next destination. Dutifully but reluctantly, Winston stepped through the doorway and was once again thrust into complete darkness to blindly face whatever fate awaited him inside. He heard the thick wooden door slam shut behind him as he had heard a thousand times before. Then he stood in the blackness of the room where he awaited his next torture.

Suddenly the room burst into light and Winston had to shield his eyes from the blinding brightness. After a few moments, when he became accustomed to the light, he looked around and was shocked to discover he was not in another stinking fetid cave filled with devices of inhuman anguish as he had anticipated, but was in a room; a real room like he recalled from life.

He was standing in a brightly lit office very similar to what he recalled his own office looking like back before he died. In fact, it was his office, he was certain of it. Winston was no longer naked, but was dressed in a casual shirt, dress pants, and expensive shoes. The office was decorated exactly like his office had been and had his same large mahogany desk and comfortable leather manager's chair positioned behind it. Winston turned to look at a certificate hanging on the wall. He was shocked to see it was his own college diploma.

"You are Mr. Winston Peter James, is that correct?" a voice said from his left. He turned to face the desk once more and saw that the chair was no longer empty, but was now occupied by a peculiar looking sort of man. The man was dressed in a business suit and sat up in a manner that appeared straight and proper, almost as if he were posturing and assuming what Winston supposed was the man's interpretation of how a businessperson should appear.

He was not however doing a very good job of looking the part he was trying to portray as his suit didn't seem to fit him well and was somewhat rumpled and disheveled. He appeared to be about middle age, slightly built with a full head of thick brown hair, which was graying somewhat at the temples, giving him a slightly distinguished look despite the issues with his attire. He wore a pair of round wire-framed glasses, which sat askew upon a long thin nose. He had a pencil thin mustache and no other facial hair. His hands were folded and resting on the top of the desk, giving Winston the impression that the man was unsure what to do with them.

Besides the obvious incongruity of the office itself being recreated in its entirety in Hell and the presence of the odd looking character behind the desk, Winston noticed there was also something else that was very wrong. It was the man's eyes. For starters, the skin around the eyes hung loosely and seemed to bag in places as if to suggest the flesh was not his own, but was some sort of skin mask worn to cover whatever countenance lie beneath it. Likewise, the man's eyes were just as strange; they did not appear to be quite human but were more cat-like and seemed to stare out at Winston without blinking.

Winston suddenly feared he might now understand what was going on. He dreadfully suspected this might be yet another new form of torture, one that would start in a place familiar to him, such as his old office, and then quickly morph into another session of agony. Cowed by his time in the countless torture chambers, Winston found himself unable to lift his head to look further at the creature. And the strange way that the creature's flesh appeared as rumpled and ill-fitting as his suit truly disturbed Winston making him certain that at any moment the scene would change and he would once again find himself the victim of an even more unimaginable torture.

The weird man repeated his request, but this time with a bit more impatience in his voice. "I asked you a question, sir! Are you Mr. Winston Peter James? Am I correct in making that assumption?" Winston could not bring himself to answer. He was not only terrified by the potential horror hiding deep inside this current scenario but had learned long ago not to willingly engage these sick creatures in conversation. He simply gave a cursory nod of acknowledgement.

"Well," the man said, "I suppose you are wondering what this is all about and why you are here with me, Winston. May I call you Winston?" Again Winston gave the slight and suspicious nod. The strange creature continued, "By the way, Winston, it is perfectly all right for you to speak to me. I realize after all you've been through while a guest here, you might be a bit reluctant. But I assure you that no harm will come to you if you choose to reply. In fact . . . I *insist* that you speak and do so immediately." There was a look of cold emotionless assertion in his cat-like eyes.

"All—all right," Winston said in a thin voice that sounded raspy and barely recognizable as the one he remembered. He had spent countless hours screaming in agony and it had been what seemed like years since he had actually had any opportunity to speak to anyone in a normal conversational voice. "Wha—what . . . is this? Why . . . why am I here?"

"Very good, Winston. Very good indeed," the being replied. Winston thought he saw the flesh mask on the creature's face slip ever so slightly. The man behind the desk said, "It's so good to have you actively participating in our conversation. It will make everything so much simpler. So please allow me to explain why I have arraigned to meet with you here. Here is the situation in a nutshell, as they say."

"I suppose you've wondered since your arrival here in our fine little corner of Hell, what it was you might have done during your lifetime to deserve such constant and relentless torture. You probably always assumed such punishment would be reserved for the lowest of the low; murders, rapists, child molesters, and so on. Am I right?"

Winston kept his eyes averted and timidly said, "Y—y—yes . . . I wondered that many times—no . . . all—all the time."

"Yes, I'm sure you have," the strange man said, and then released a loud guffaw of laughter, sending the most ungodly foul stench across the desk between them and directly into Winston's face. Winston felt his stomach turn over with revulsion at the smell of the vile stink. He noticed once again how the strange man's hands never left the top of the desk, making Winston wonder if those hands might be fused together into that pose to make whatever lurked inside that bizarre skin seem more human. Winston's eyes were focused on those hands and he thought for a moment that he saw maggots crawling between the intertwined fingers.

"NOW PAY ATTENTION, WINSTON!" the being shouted, momentarily losing his composure only to quickly regain it once again and instantly return to his calm, business-like demeanor. "Let's cut to the chase, shall we?"

Winston nodded silently once again, then realizing he had not spoken as requested, he quickly said, "Y—yes . . . please."

The man said, "All right then," and he proceeded to explain. "Well, Winston, it appears there was a slight clerical error, which resulted in your coming here. You see, as it works out, you are actually not supposed to be here after all."

Winston felt his heart thudding in his chest. He thought to himself, How could that possibly be? Could I have really been made to suffer all this time over a simple clerical error?

"Cl—clerical . . . error?" Winston asked cautiously, not believing it was possible.

"Yes. I'm afraid so," the man replied nonchalantly."

"Wha—what do you mean?" he asked, confused.

"You see, every so often, the equivalent of one thousand or more earth years, we do an audit of our guests to makes sure there have been no mistakes. And if we do discover mistakes we do our best to try to make them right immediately."

Winston asked with a bit of uncertainty, "Mistakes?"

"Yes, mistakes," the being replied. "You see, here in Hell we aren't perfect; nor are we expected to be. Those sort of high and mighty expectations are reserved for that other place." He cast his eyes upward. "Down here we sometimes have the occasional unplanned faux pas, if you pardon my French. In other words, we have been known to make mistakes."

"Mistake." Winston repeated now as a statement rather than a question. He had no idea where this bizarre conversation might be heading, but he had a very uncomfortable feeling about it.

The creature behind the desk replied, "It appears you, Winston, have been the subject of our latest unfortunate situation. Winston expected the man to raise his hands and simulate air quotes when he said the word "situation," but he did not. He suspected the creature before him might not be able to move his hands at all. The longer Winston studied him the more he realized the thing was not a man but perhaps a higher level demon of greater intelligence than most he had encountered and was wearing some sort of suit apparently made of human flesh to make himself seem less offensive. Winston wondered why a place which had subjected him to countless bouts of humiliation and torture would even bother with such a ruse. It made no logical sense to him, but little had made sense in this place since his arrival.

The being said, "So as I said, it appears you not only are not supposed to be here, but I am sorry to say you are not even supposed to be dead."

"W—what?" Winston managed to stammer. "N—not supposed to be dead?"

"Yes," the creature replied. "But that particular fact is somewhat irrelevant as you are now both dead and here as well. It appears what happened was one of our minions who was sent to retrieve the souls of the dead—I believe you call them Grim Reapers in your world—mistakenly brought you to us instead of the human he was sent to retrieve. The error was only discovered a short while ago during a routine audit. You will be happy to know the minion who made that particular mistake is currently being punished for his failure, and I'm certain you can scarcely imagine what we are doing to *him*."

Before Winston could reply, not that he had any idea what to say anyway, the creature asked him, "Do you happen to recall exactly how you died?"

Winston most certainly did recall every detail of his death just as he remembered every single agonizing moment of every torture he had endured since his arrival in Hell.

"Shot." Winston replied, "I was shot during a mugging . . . a robbery."

"Yes, that is correct," the strange being said. "You were shot while being robbed by a very bad human named Wilson Johns, a man who you may recall was about your same age and physical build. You were supposed to overpower him and he was supposed end up dead, but our soul retriever incorrectly interfered and the result was you are here and he is not. "

"But . . . but how?" Winston asked, "How could this have happened?"

The creature explained, "Actually, I see very clearly how something like this might have occurred. Think about it. Two men, physically similar; one Winston James the other Wilson Johns; it makes perfect sense to me. Besides, after a few millennia, all human beings start to look alike to us."

Winston could feel the anger and hatred build inside him. With more forcefulness than he would have believed possible he asked, "You mean to tell me that worthless bastard has been alive, robbing, killing, raping and whatever else he chooses to do while I've been suffering unimaginable tortures, which were really meant for him? Is that what you're saying?"

The creature looked directly at Winston with his strange, cat-like eyes and replied, "Yes. I'm sorry to say that is exactly what the situation is. So you can see why we are all a bit embarrassed by this unfortunate oversight."

"Embarrassed? Oversight?" Winston said in a louder voice than he had used in a very, very long time. "This is not an oversight. That is . . . well . . . I don't know what the hell to call it."

"Yes. You are most certainly correct and have a right to be upset." The being agreed, "And unfortunately, it's like trying to un-ring a bell. There is nothing we can do to restore you to life. You are dead and will remain so. However, there might be something we can do to help you get revenge against the man you was responsible for killing you in the first place."

Winston looked directly at the creature, suddenly interested. He was furious and if he had an opportunity to right this injustice he would jump at the chance do so. Then perhaps the man who murdered him would be forced to spend eternity along the Path while Winston could move on to whatever place, presumably less painful than this, he was meant to be.

"How?" Winston asked eagerly. "How can I do this? What do I have to do?"

The creature gave Winston a sly look and said, "On earth it is currently October 31, Halloween night, the night of the dead. It is the one time during the year when we are permitted to allow certain souls to return to earth to take care of any unfinished business, or to do special tasks on Hell's behalf. We have made arrangements for you to return to earth for one night to retrieve the soul of Wilson Johns and bring him back here to us.

Once this job is done you will move on to another place, not heaven—you were never good enough for that, few are —but another place much less unpleasant than this particular section of Hell. All you have to do is return to the world of the living, confront Wilson Johns, take this special dagger, and plunge it into his heart." Suddenly a long sharp knife appeared in Winston's hand. "You do that and we will do the rest."

"But . . . but, I can't do that . . . I'm not a killer. I've no idea how to do such a thing." Winston explained his hand uncomfortably gripping the handle of the dagger.

Looking perturbed the creature said, "Well, Winston. We are sending you back to get Wilson Johns. You will only have a few earth hours to do what must be done then you will be returned to us. If you come back empty handed, you will return to where you left off on the Path and will continue serving out a punishment rightfully meant for someone else. The choice is entirely yours."

A moment later, Winston found himself standing in an alley in a city that looked very familiar to him. He was wearing the same clothing he had been wearing the night he died. In fact, this alley was the very same alley he had tried to use as a shortcut when Wilson Johns had attacked, robbed, and murdered him.

In the distance he saw someone entering the alley. As the stranger came briefly into the glow of a nearby streetlight, Winston was shocked to see it was no stranger but was him as he had looked the night he died. He then realized that the strange creature had returned him to earth on the exact night he had been murdered. Winston hadn't been murdered on Halloween night but that didn't seem to matter in the strange juxtaposition of time that seemed to exist between the two worlds.

As the Winston of earth approached the ethereal Winston a man dressed in dark clothing suddenly sprang from the shadows. Winston realized it was all happening again and this time Winston was about to actually see himself being murdered. Reacting, not thinking, Winston forced his spiritual self into his earthly body just as Wilson Johns raised his gun and fired. Simultaneously the spirit of Winston lifted his physical right hand and plunged the invisible dagger deep into the mugger's chest, piercing his heart.

Wilson Johns let out a howl and fell to the ground in a dead heap. Winston James floated out of his physical body and stood nearby. From the fallen form of Johns rose a stream of tiny red sparkling glowing lights, which began to flow into the blade of the dagger, causing it to illuminate in a crimson light. Winston knew this was what he had to take back to Hell with him to make things right. He looked down and saw his own dead earthly body lying on the ground. The creature had told Winston he could not undo what had been done, but could only try to make things right.

Without warning Winston started to slowly fade from the world of the living, and within a moment, found himself back in the room that looked like his old office, the dagger still held tightly in his hand.

The strange being was still seated behind the desk with it fleshy gloved hands folded in front of him. "Very good work, Winston. I see you have brought back the knife and have acquired the soul we needed to right this injustice perpetrated on you." The knife disappeared from Winston's hand the rematerialized on the top of the desk. The creature's hands did not move to pick it up.

"Yes . . . yes, I have," Winston said, still quite shaken from all that had happened. "I've done what you asked. Now Johns can be punished as you require and I can move on to wherever it is I have earned the right to move on to."

"Well," the creature said hesitantly, "about that . . . well, there's a bit of a problem."

"What are you talking about?" Winston said, now with an air of defiance. "You said I didn't deserve to be here, that I was put here by mistake, and that I could move on to another place."

The creature wavered then said, "Well, yes. But that was before you returned to your world and killed Wilson Johns. Now, my dear Winston James, you are officially a murderer."

"But I did that for you. I was carrying out your orders. I killed for you. If I didn't do what you said I was going to have to continue down the Path," Winston said angrily.

"True, but the final decision to actually kill Johns was yours to make," the creature said. "And that made you a killer. You had your revenge and you enjoyed it as well. The Path is exactly where murderers belong. It appears, my good Winston, as if you were damned if you did and damned if you didn't."

Then, before Winston had a chance to protest further, he found himself once again outside on the Path. He looked out at the endless road before him, hung his head in sorrow as he listened to the waling of the tortured souls and slowly began to trudge along the Path to his next stop.

It Came Upon a Midnight Clear

*'It matters little,' she said, softly. 'To you, very little.
Another idol has displaced me; and if it can cheer and
comfort you in time to come, as I would have tried to do, I
have no just cause to grieve.'*
—Charles Dickens, *A Christmas Carol*

The solitary automobile moved slowly along the empty
main street of town. The man behind the wheel was paying
little if any attention to the darkened storefronts or to the
virtually abandoned thoroughfare. It was after 11:15 pm
and although he was heading home, his mind was still
back at the office where it always seemed to be. His
thoughts were obsessed with important issues, which
should have been resolved long before he chose to leave for
the night. Then again, there were always critical issues
needing resolution, and he knew even if he worked twenty-
four hours a day, seven days a week he still would never be
able to take care of all of them. It seemed for every single
problem he managed to rectify three more came forward to
take their place. But he supposed such was his lot in life.

The night was very clear and every star could be seen
for miles in the cloudless Pennsylvania sky. The
temperature was surprisingly mild for December twenty-
fourth, Christmas Eve. For those local residents hoping for
a white Christmas, the pleasant temperatures would likely
prove somewhat disappointing. Fifty-six-year-old Evan
Flint had no need for Christmas, no desire to celebrate the
holiday, or for that matter, no one with whom to share it
had he chosen to do so. At first glance, one might think
Evan had everything a man could want out of life, being
the richest man in the county if not the state. And if
someone were to ask him, Evan would likely agree and say
that he was quite satisfied with his life, stating
categorically that he had absolutely no need for a wife,

children, close friends or other such things he often referred to as "trappings of life." Evan had more money than he could spend in three lifetimes and his fortune continued to grow daily. But he was completely unaware that in such a reply he would be lying not only to the questioner but more importantly to himself.

Evan was the sole owner of a manufacturing company located on the outskirts of the small Schuylkill County, Pennsylvania town of Ashton. The factory employed well over two thousand residents from all over the county. It was one of the few remaining manufacturing facilities where one could at least attempt to earn a decent living. For most of the workers the factory felt more like a prison and for many of them who were saddled with financial difficulties, a prison was exactly what the place had become. Those residents who had overextended their credit or had lost what few savings they had during the downturn in the economy had little choice but to tolerate the meager pay and substandard working conditions offered at Flint Manufacturing.

The benefits Evan offered were equally substandard and even though he knew about his workers pitifully struggling to make ends meet he had no qualms whatsoever about taking advantage of each and every one of them. He realized if the economy were good and there were plenty of other places to find profitable employment he would likely lose many of his better qualified employees. Yes, he was certain most of them would leave to seek employment elsewhere. But fortunately for Evan, with the economy in the toilet he could treat his workers however he pleased. To say the least, not many of Flint Manufacturing's workers could be described as satisfied employees.

Evan was well aware of the workers' complaints as well as the various derogatory nicknames they had devised for him and called him behind his back, such as Evan-eezer or Skin Flint. Evan did not think of himself as such a tightwad, but considered his economic philosophy to be conservatively frugal. When he first heard of the names, Evan had been furious and had fired a handful of workers who he had determined to be responsible for starting the whole mess. He was able to identify those people thanks to a few of his loyal cronies and suck-ups who could be counted on to bring him all the latest dirt.

But one thing that always seemed to be true of such negative nicknames was that once they were spoken aloud, they seemed to stick—and stick forever. Such was the case with the names they applied to Evan. And soon it became apparent to Evan that he would either have to learn to ignore the snide remarks and derogatory name-calling or else he would have to fire his entire workforce.

The one particular term, which seemed to bother him the most, was Evan-eezer. That name really irked him because it summed up the complete lack of gratitude his workforce felt toward him. He could not understand what was wrong with them. He had managed to keep all of them employed during some of the most difficult economic times in the history of the state.

Although he didn't like the idea of being lumped in with such a miserly Dickensian stereotype, if Evan had taken the time to consider the possibility, he might soon discover his own life actually had many similar parallels to that of the fictitious infamous Mr. Scrooge.

Like Scrooge, Evan was a loner as a child with few if any friends. As a young man in college, he had met, fallen in love with, and married a beautiful young woman—whose name was Claire. Eventually Evan's true love left him just as Scrooge's had in the story.

Evan had started his manufacturing company as a partnership with a young man named Jack Worley. In *A Christmas Carol*, Scrooge had started his company with his partner Jacob Marley. Scrooge's partner died, leaving him to run the business alone. A similar thing happened to Jack Worley.

Evan had always been certain that someday his partnership with Jack would end one way or another. He had assumed this from the very start because the two were opposites. Whereas Evan had come from nothing and worked long hours and most weekends to build the business, his partner Jack had come from old money and was known throughout the area as a reckless playboy. Though it was true that Jack had put up the initial startup money for the company, he had no real interest in running the business itself and was glad to leave the day-to-day affairs to Evan. But Jack's shiftless behavior nonetheless irritated him. Evan's marriage ended after just a few short years when Claire tired of the long hours he spent at work. Evan explained that he was only working so hard to build a future for the two of them, but that did nothing to appease her. She felt she had no need for money or the finer things of life. She simply wanted the man she married to be there for her when she needed him and Evan was never there. On the day she left, Claire told him his true love was not really her, but his money and the power that money brought to him. Scrooge's lost love had told him, "Another idol has displaced me; and if it can cheer and comfort you in time to come, as I would have tried to do, I have no just cause to grieve."

After Claire left him, Evan immersed himself even further into his work, having nothing else to fill his empty hours. Within a few short years, he had singlehandedly built the manufacturing company to a booming business employing over one thousand people. While other companies were closing and sending their products overseas to be manufactured, Evan's company was growing and expanding and continuing to hire more workers weekly.

While Evan was busy working, Jack did virtually nothing to contribute to the business. Instead, he continued his wild and carefree ways, all the time taking his share of the profits. Evan knew that somehow Jack's reckless behavior had to come to an end, and it was likely going to be left to Evan to find a way to stop Jack. Then one day Jack was killed in a tragic boating accident. The man had been sailing off the New Jersey coast, having a private party on his favorite boat with several young coeds, when a freak explosion killed him as well as all of his passengers.

An investigation into the accident was started and for quite some time police closely scrutinized Evan Flint, considering him a person of more than just casual interest in the incident. Although the authorities had never gotten so far as to arrest Evan, accuse him of murder, or even refer to the inquiry as a murder investigation, they did comment that the events surrounding the accident were suspicious. They were likewise reluctant to label the incident as an accidental death.

Their suspicions likely arose when they questioned Evan and he did not even bother to feign the slightest bit of sadness at the loss of his partner. He even stated that as far as he was concerned, it was some sort of cosmic divine intervention and that Jack had gotten exactly what he deserved. To a police investigator that statement alone would set off all sorts of internal alarms.

But it was later when the police discovered that the two partners had taken out substantial life insurance policies at the time the business was formed—each naming the other as sole beneficiary of those funds—that they believed they had a motive and truly became suspicious.

The insurance policies were each worth five million dollars each and with Jack's death the entire sum went to Evan. Police felt that this fact alone would have been motive enough for Evan wanting his partner dead. But they also learned from questioning some of Evan's employees that there was no love lost between the two partners.

Regardless of what their suspicions might have been, following a thorough police investigation, it was determined that although Jack's death could very well have been a planned murder, it was more likely just an unavoidable accident. There were far fewer facts pointing to murder than to an accident so the police had little choice but to reluctantly drop that particular avenue of investigation. In the eyes of several of the investigators, Evan was never completely exonerated but since the affair was officially ruled accidental there was nothing more they could do. And so Evan was free to collect the insurance money.

But the townspeople and the many workers at his factory were far from satisfied with the authorities' findings. They had watched Evan and Jack interact for years and they believed Evan was a control freak and they thought they knew just how far Evan would go to get his way. And as much as they disliked Evan with his sullen, much too serious disposition, they all seemed to have loved Jack Worley with his outwardly friendly personality. Many of them were certain that Evan was perfectly capable of systematically planning and carrying out the murder of his partner. They also believed he would care nothing for the other guests caught in the accident as collateral damage. If they were given the choice, most of them would have preferred if it had been Evan who had died instead of Jack.

They all had many reasons to hate Evan and had tried on many occasions to unionize their workforce. But each time Evan had managed to successfully fight back those attempts to bring in labor unions. His employees didn't know how Evan was able to keep the union out but some of them suspected he might have greased the right palms or perhaps used some other form of coercion.

Evan was always on the lookout for union organizers. As he drove and thought about the events of the day, Evan's major concern was that his latest planned change in the company's benefits package might push his workforce too far. He worried that if they tried to unionize again, he might not be able to keep them out. Evan had some underlying discomfort that very possibly his next move might open a door to potential labor union organization. One benefit his workers still enjoyed, which most companies had abandoned many years earlier, was a pension plan. But now Evan had decided he would have to take drastic measures to keep his company competitive with offshore manufacturers and keep his own personal fortune growing as well. The result was that he had decided to do away with the company pension plan. He would essentially freeze the pension, so no one would lose any time and monetary benefits they had accrued to date, but he would not support any additional contributions to the plan. From March or April of the next year on, he would institute a 401K savings plan where employees could put in their own money to save and thereby manage their own retirement funds. The idea made perfect sense to Evan, plus it would save his company a ton of money.

Both Evan's company controller and vice president of manufacturing tried to change his mind about the move, complaining that not only would it further hurt employee morale but it might also cause a mass exodus of workers from the company. Evan knew that although the workers would complain as usual, there was no way they would consider walking out during such a hostile economic climate. Perhaps in a few years, if the economy started to recover they might think about it, but by then the initial pain from the change would be long forgotten. Besides, he was familiar with every company within fifty miles and was confident not a single one of them still had a pension plan either.

The reason Evan was currently feeling stressed was likely because of an argument he had with his two top executives earlier in the day on that very subject. Evan banded his hand against the steering wheel shouting "Screw 'em all! I'm the owner of this company as well as its CEO and my word is gospel. I am the only one looking out for my employees' futures. I founded this company; that makes me the creator, which means as far as they all are concerned I am God. And if I say this is how things are going to be, then so be it."

Evan suddenly felt a strange and slightly painful sensation inside his head as if he might be on the verge of getting a severe headache. "No wonder," Evan thought aloud, certain he understood the reason for the headache. "After the frustrating day I just had I'm not at all surprised."

Since the next day was Christmas, all of his workers were off for one day for the holiday but would be returning to work December 26th. A large number of them had saved vacation for the time between Christmas and New Years Day but most would be back at work. And Evan, of course would also be at work as well. He planned to make the announcement about his pension plan change through the company's official communication channels first thing the start of the next business day. He chuckled to himself thinking about what a terrible Christmas present they would all be receiving this year; especially the workers who were off for the holiday and might not learn about it until they returned, which was also fine with Evan.

Once again, he felt the slight pain in his skull and made a mental note to take some painkillers when he arrived home. Since he planned on doing nothing special for the rest of the evening, he decided he would treat himself to a nightcap as well.

Soon Evan had passed through town and was on a rural road heading out into the country toward his estate. He turned into his driveway and paused in front of the eight foot ornately decorated iron gates blocking his access. Pressing a button on his remote control unit the gates swung invitingly open and he continued up his long driveway, the gates closing automatically behind him. As Evan approached the front of his luxurious three-story brick mansion, he pressed another button and watched the first of four huge garage doors open.

Closing the garage door behind him, Evan entered the kitchen area of his home and quickly typed in his security code to suppress the shrill scream of the alarm system. The house was suddenly thrust into blessed silence.

Evan walked into the living room and pressed a button on a control console illuminating a reading light behind a large leather chair across the room. He glanced at the tall, ornately-carved grandfather clock he had purchased from a clockmaker in Switzerland; the time was now 11:25 pm.

Then with the press of another button the large gas fireplace burst into flames, washing the room with its glow and comforting warmth. Evan walked over to a bar next to the fireplace and poured himself a large glass of whiskey over ice. He sat down on the chair, allowing himself to sink deeply into the leather upholstery. After a few long swigs of his nightcap, Evan's mind began to wander back to a much happier time, back to a time when he and Claire had been married and were still so madly in love. Back then Evan always looked forward to coming home from work and finding her there.

During those years they had no money and lived in a small apartment above a pharmacy on the main street of town. He always promised Claire that someday they would have more money then she could imagine, but she never seemed to care. And on the day she left, he finally understood, much too late, that she didn't want things but only wanted him. He recalled how he had begged and pleaded with her to stay swearing he would find a way to change his work habits, but she said that she knew better.

Evan was simply the way he was, and there was nothing she or anyone else could do to change him.

Evan later learned Claire had remarried a few years after the divorce and the last he heard, she had been living in another state. Claire apparently now had four grown children and a herd of grandchildren. He supposed she was happy in her new life but he truly seldom thought much about her, except at quiet times such as the one he currently was experiencing. Evan had his company, his employees, and his money. As such, he insisted he had all he could possibly need out of life. But sometimes he still felt so very bitter and angry over the loss of his wife.

He liked to be in charge and to control every aspect of his life. Claire's leaving had been a major blow to him emotionally. But it had also bothered him on another level. It irritated him that he could not control Claire and make her stay with him. That was also how he had felt about his late partner, Jack. But now that situation was well under control.

No longer wanting to dwell on the painful memories of his past, Evan finished off his drink, poured himself another, took several long generous sips then grabbed the TV remote control for the sixty-inch flat screen mounted above the mahogany fireplace mantel and turned it on. He mindlessly surfed from channel to channel, hoping for something to stir his interest.

After a while, he stopped at a channel, which was playing the 1938 classic black and white film adaptation of Charles Dickens' *A Christmas Carol*. The scene currently showing depicted Jacob Marley's ghost howling and rattling his chains madly as only one suffering the tortures of an eternity in Hell could do.

"Bah Humbug!" Evan said, chuckling to himself enjoying the way he was lampooning the Christmas classic and already feeling the effects of the whiskey. In frustration he pressed the off button on the TV remote and the giant screen went black. He sat quietly in his large chair and finished his drink, sitting and staring at the flames dancing in the fireplace.

After a bit Evan thought he saw something in the flames. It had only been there for a fleeting moment but what he saw seemed as clear in his mind as if it had been there for hours. He thought he saw the face of Jack Worley grinning madly out at him as the fire charred and melted the flesh from his skull. Then the hideous creatures mouth began to slowly open and Evan knew the next thing he would hear would be he own name being spoken in some ghastly undead voice. He quickly shook his head to clear his mind of the horrible image and thankfully it disappeared. His head now hurt worse than before. Something was wrong with him and Evan realized he might have to visit his doctor in a few days.

After a moment, he got to his feet and discovered he was surprisingly off kilter. He had not expected to become so drunk so quickly but thinking back, he realized he had not eaten since breakfast. No wonder he was half hammered. No wonder he was imagining things. Suddenly he was startled by the sound of the grandfather clock striking midnight. "Time for bed," he said to the empty room

As he regained his balance and attempted to stagger out toward the hallway, he heard a strange noise coming from the foyer, out near the front door. It was then he realized that he had disarmed the security system when he got home but he had forgotten to rearm it. He began to wonder if some low-life scumbag of a character from town had taken it upon himself to attempt to break in and rob him. If that were the case, Evan was prepared to give the criminal a present he had never anticipated. He walked over to the fireplace and clumsily withdrew a large wrought-iron poker with a menacing looking tip. Holding the doorframe for support, he slowly peered around the corner to look out toward the front door.

What he saw caught him completely by surprise. There was no would-be burglar skulking inside the door, in fact the entire hallway was empty; at least he initially thought it was empty. Then Evan noticed something strange starting to occur. It was as if the air in the hall closest to the door was changing its physical properties. It seemed at first to shimmer then to ripple in almost liquid undulations appearing like waves above a blacktop roadway on a hot summer day. Then a shape began forming within the distorted air.

It appeared to be some sort of mass, low to the floor, perhaps only two feet high at its apex in the center then tapering downward on sides forming an elliptical series of pulsating and bubbling globs. At first, it reminded Evan of an enormous fried egg with a large flesh-colored dome in the center instead of a yolk. In fact, the entire thing seemed to be flesh-like not only in color but in the apparent texture of its skin. The mass was in constant motion, undulating and bubbling wildly. After a few moments, the waves of air stopped and the thing in the hall seemed to solidify and become real.

"What the hell!" Evan exclaimed in shock raising the poker high above his head, prepared to lash out at the strange living nightmare just a few feet in front of him. Suddenly the rhythmically pulsing shape began to move toward him under some form of propulsion he could not begin to comprehend. As it got closer, Evan could see large spidery veins, some as thick as rope, moving throughout its hideous form. It was then he noticed a disgustingly foul stench emanating from the strange being. It made his stomach turn with revulsion, the thing smelling like a long-dead rotting carcass.

At first he took a cautious step away from the vile creature; then driven by a courage brought on from either the whiskey or simple stupidity, he decided to lunge forward with the poker and attack the thing. He plunged the sharp end of the poker deep into the front side of the mass, close to the large center dome. He let go of the handle out of sheer disgust upon feeling the unearthly consistency of the thing. The poker seemed to sink deep into the throbbing glob of vein-riddled flesh then spring harmlessly back out and fall to the floor with a clank that echoed in the empty hallway.

Evan was suddenly hit with an incredible pain in the center of his own gut, which doubled him over for a moment, before it began to slowly subside and he could once again stand semi-erect. It was as if he were being made to feel the pain that he had meant to inflict on the horrifying creeping entity.

He staggered backward a step or two and wondered aloud, "What manner of creature is this ungodly thing?" He started to turn to run for the back door when suddenly he heard a soft, liquidy voice calling from behind him, "Evan . . . Where . . . do you think . . . you are going?"

He stopped in his tracks and turned around slowly, convinced that the hideous twitching blob on his hallway floor had just impossibly spoken to him. "Wha—what?" He stammered.

"There's no need to run, Evan . . . Yes . . . That's right . . . I know who you are . . . as I should," the thing seemed to say to him, although he couldn't quite make out any mechanism by which the creature had articulated the words. Then he thought he noticed a long slit forming in the center of the creature's dome, appearing to run vertically rather than horizontally. Although Evan realized since the creature was almost round in shape, he had no way of knowing what was its front, side, or back.

The crack opened slightly and the stench that had originally accosted him became even more repugnant. Then he saw the slit begin to vibrate as he heard the quivering voice once again, "So, Evan . . . What special plans do you have for this lovely Christmas Eve?" Evan was taken aback by the question, feeling it quite odd and perhaps not what he would have expected the thing to ask him. Then again, what was happening was so bizarre he truly had no idea what he should expect.

The vile thing asked, "Where are your friends, Evan? Where is the merriment . . . the festivity . . . where is all the joyous celebration?"

Evan was confused beyond comprehension and although he felt foolish doing so he shouted angrily at the pulsating gelatinous mass, "Who, or what the hell are you? What manner of being are you? And why in the name of all that's holy are you here?"

Once again the long slit began to vibrate, resembling the wave of an oscilloscope as the foul odor once again permeated the room and Evan heard the strange voice speak. "Why, Evan! Do you mean to say . . . you don't know who I am? Don't you recognize me?"

"What in the name of God are you talking about?" Evan shouted. "You are one of the most horrible looking things I have ever seen, even more revolting than the creatures of my worst nightmares. Recognize you? I don't even know what manner of being you are! For all I know you may just be a figment of my imagination. Maybe in reality, I am actually back there asleep in the chair and dreaming all of this." He pointed back toward the living room.

The blob-like gelatinous mound slid stealthily closer to the unsuspecting Evan, who was too preoccupied and equally confused to notice the thing's approach and as such did not step back. The creature continued speaking to him with a calm and almost hypnotic tone. "Tonight is Christmas Eve . . . and you should be spending it with your loved ones, Evan . . . not sitting in the dark in this self-imposed prison you call a home . . . but then again . . . you have no loved ones do you, Evan?"

Now Evan was becoming angry, at least to the extent his revulsion would permit. His discomfort was rapidly replaced by his more typical arrogant attitude; one he had developed throughout his lifetime and an attitude with which he was most comfortable. "What do you know of me you hideous blob? Nothing! You are just some sort of mirage, an illusion."

Then sounding once again very much like Ebenezer Scrooge, Evan said "You are nothing more than the result of too little food and too much drink. Hell, by tomorrow morning I probably won't remember any of this . . . this strange dream. You are but a disgusting apparition. Leave me at once!"

"On the contrary," the thing corrected, "I won't be going anywhere . . . at least not yet. You do understand, Evan, that Christmas Eve is a special time . . . a time for magic and a time for miracles. And after tonight, things will never be the same for you. Look closer at me, Evan . . . is there truly nothing . . . not even one little thing about me . . . that seems familiar to you?"

Evan stared more closely at the loathsome slimy rippling mass of veins and flesh, and although he knew he had never seen anything like it ever before there was a feeling, a presence about the creature that really did seem somewhat familiar. Somehow there actually was something about the unbelievable abomination that he did seem to recognize, or he at least he seemed to sense some sort of indescribable understanding. It was not something about the creature's appearance as that was truly abhorrent, but it was something less tangible he seemed to feel; something almost telepathic.

"Ah!" The mass said through its rippling slit of a mouth. "There is some recognition after all . . . do you care to venture a guess about my origin, Evan? Do you have the nerve to try?" The creature slid even closer to the unsuspecting man.

Then suddenly the realization hit Evan and he understood everything. "You—are you insinuating . . . are you trying to tell me you are . . . me?"

"That's right, Evan," the blob said. "In a manner of speaking . . . I am you. You see, I am actually the physical manifestation of your own tainted immortal soul. I am the essence of you, Evan . . . this is what you have become inside . . . a vile, disgusting mass of anger, hatred and bitterness . . . no love or kindness or beauty exists in me . . . because such traits no longer exist in you. You have become like a living disease . . . a foul blight on the face of the earth . . . all you care about is yourself and your precious money. Your own wife, Claire, was right, Evan . . . she left you because she knew you could only have one true love in your life . . . and your love is your insatiable desire for money."

"It can't be," Evan screamed. "It's impossible! You can't possibly be me. You're nothing like me. You are just some horrible figment born of too much whiskey. Leave my house now. I demand it."

He made a drunken futile gesture pointing his hand toward the front door. It was then that he realized the massive globule was now just inches away from him.

"I'll be going nowhere just yet, Evan," the thing said "Look at me, Evan . . . I am your murderous soul made manifest."

Evan looked as if he had been struck with a club. "Murderous?" he asked. "What are you talking about? Jack? Are you talking about Jack Worley's death? The boating accident? You stupid pile of stinking flesh! That was an accident I tell you!"

The thing slid yet closer until the outer edge of its flattest surface was touching the toe of Evan's shoe. Then it spoke again. "You can lie to the police, Evan . . . and you can lie to the townspeople . . . you can never lie to yourself, Evan . . . and I am you inner most murderous self."

With that, Evan tried to back away, but before he could make a single step a long, thin, ropelike tongue shot out from the mouth slit and wrapped itself tightly around Evan's neck. It burned the skin on his neck and Evan could feel his breath being cut off by the fleshy lasso. Then the ropy tongue began to retract into the creature as the slit of a mouth grew in size from just a few inches to more than a foot and a half in length.

Evan was pulled toward the slit gasping for air and whimpering with pain and realization. This thing, this abomination really was formed from the most evil and most horrendous essence, from the very core of his tainted soul. And this unspeakable inside-out version of himself was sent here from Hell to claim him; to make Evan one with its own grotesquery.

Then the sides of the gaping maw separated opening to reveal an enormous black orifice. The blackness seemed bottomless; as if it were not so much a mouth, but an opening or a passageway to some unimaginably horrible place.

Before he realized it, Evan's head was inside the thing's mouth, which closed tightly around his shoulders. His flesh boiled and bubbled beneath its slimy touch. Soon Evan's pitiful cries became muffled and were finally silenced. The sides of the slit rippled even more frantically slowly working the rest of Evan's twitching body further inside. His body thrashed and flayed as it was sucked deeper inside the beast. Within a few short moments, Evan Flint was completely gone.

The creature remained in the hallway for a few more moments; then it slowly faded from sight until it was completely gone along with the man whose greed had made the creature's temporary existence necessary on that clear and magical Christmas Eve.

Mill Monster:
A Ghost Story

Besides black art, there is only automation and mechanization.
—Federico Garcia Lorca

Nobody knows whether our personalities pass on to another existence or sphere, but if we can evolve an instrument so delicate to be manipulated by our personality as it survives in the next life such an instrument ought to record something . . .
—Thomas Edison, 1928

The aged rusting hulk sat in the back of an unlit, seldom used section of the machine shop, looking like the decaying remains of some giant once-great weapon of war. Its olive drab paint had long since become flaked and chipped. The decals which once bore its machine number, #137 and its model name "Mill Master," were now barely legible.

The same was true of its other decal, the special one that had been purchased and placed on the side of the machine as a token of endearment by its long time operator so many years ago. The decal depicted a stylized cartoon of the machine in action, its huge caricature mouth filled with gleaming white teeth in the process of ripping bars of metal to shreds. And beneath the sketch in large horror-movie style font characters were the words "Mill Monster."

The machine had been one of the first computer controlled machining centers in the factory, purchased brand new in the mid-1960s, when the owner, Nate Bartinski was still a young, forward thinking engineer determined to make something of the failing factory his father had left to him when he passed away. Nate graduated from the Pennsylvania State University with a degree in Industrial Engineering and had just started working full-time at the plant with his father when Nate Senior was struck dead with a massive coronary at the age of fifty-five.

Nate Jr. was no stranger to manufacturing, having been raised around machinery and having worked every summer and every break from school in his father's plant since the age of sixteen. But suddenly he found himself in the unfamiliar role of factory manager and he had to quickly adapt and learn to survive in order to protect the jobs of the fifty-three men employed at Bartinski Manufacturing at that time. The plant was located at the west end of the Schuylkill County town of Ashton, Pennsylvania.

Taking over operation more out of necessity than desire, Nate quickly began to modernize the facility in every way possible. He learned about some new technology called Numerical Control or NC machinery. Although the technology was new to him and other small-size manufacturers, it had been in use since the early 1950s by those larger manufacturers with military contracts. He learned of the machinery because Bartinski Manufacturing made most of its money from military work so he had many contacts throughout the field.

He decided he needed to bring this modern technology into his plant, and with a line of credit from the Ashton National Bank he purchased the American made Mill Master in the summer of 1968.

In its day, the Mill Master was considered state-of-the-art technology. It could perform the work of five men running traditional manual machines. Although the motivation for most companies who purchased such equipment was to eliminate jobs; this was not the case with Nate Bartinski. He was looking not only for ways to keep his current workforce, but to help them to become more productive so he could to purchase more machines and hire more employees. He knew he would be able to not just save his father's business, but grow it as well.

And as things worked out, his plan was very successful. The Mill Master was capable of cutting through metal easily and when it was in production, shredded hot metal chips flew through the air and piled high on the floor around it. This was at a time before machine enclosures and protective guards, so the machine operator had to be on the alert for red-hot flying shards. The machine's cutters sounded like a growling beast as the milled away layer after layer of steel. This was how it got its nickname "Mill Monster."

Its first operator was a young man about Nate's age by the name of Joseph DeNunzio. Joseph was the first generation American son of two Italian immigrant parents. Although he was the man with the lowest seniority in the shop, he got the job because he was young and was not afraid to attempt to master the new technology. Most of the older machinists who had worked their entire careers on manual equipment had no desire to become involved in such "new-fangled equipment"; no matter how many times Nate tried to tell them it was the way of the future. He believed that the new technology would soon replace most if not all of what they thought of as conventional machines. And he had been correct.

The Mill Master was controlled by means of a computer program punched onto a one inch Mylar tape placed in a tape reader. Since they had no one with the knowledge of how to write programs for the machine, Joseph volunteered to learn how to do so. He took the programming manuals home and after a few days he began punching out programs on a tape preparation device Nate had purchased for him. And from then on, the Mill Master began making Nate's company money, and lots of it.

Joseph took quickly to the machine and to programming, and within no time at all he had it chomping its way through part after part making precise, accurate, and repetitive components of the highest quality. The more Joseph used the machine the more proficient he became. He loved working with the equipment, and with Nate's permission and using his own money, Joseph designed and had the special Mill Monster decal made placing it proudly on the side of the machine.

As the years went by Joseph's skill grew, as did the company's profits, and soon Nate was able to purchase other computer-controlled machines, each one more sophisticated than the last. Within a few years, the technology of the new machines quickly made the Mill Master seem antiquated. With the advent of mini and microcomputer technology as well as Computer Numerical Control or CNC machines, the Mill Master soon was considered obsolete. However, it still had its place with the company and continued to manufacture the same parts it had been making for many years.

Although he worked with and programmed all of the new equipment, Joseph never had the same attraction to any of these as he had to the Mill Monster. It was his first machine and as such, held a special place in his heart. Then when the invasion of dramatically inexpensive Japanese CNC machines hit in the late 1970s to 1980s virtually wiping out all U.S. machine tool builders, Joseph found himself becoming frustrated with the lack of quality in so many of the new pieces of equipment from overseas. Joseph had done his best to try to talk Nate out of buying the foreign equipment. But as Nate had explained, every year more U.S. machine tool manufacturers disappeared, while the quality of the foreign machines continued to improve at an exponential rate. Eventually they soon had little choice but to accept the reality and buy what was available.

"Joe, you surely know I would love nothing better than to buy only U.S. made equipment, but my hands are tied here," Nate had told him. "Most of our favorite domestic machine tool builders have gone belly-up; and even finding replacement parts for our current machines is becoming a nightmare."

Joseph conceded, "Yeah, I know what we are going through but it still makes me sick to my stomach to see the way the entire U.S. machine tool industry is just vanishing. The imported stuff, even the best of it, can't compare with what we used to get stateside."

Even though Nate's company was not in any danger of losing work to the many new manufacturing companies opening up around the world, because he primarily dealt with military work, many U. S. manufacturers who already had lost work to foreign companies were now starting to bid against his company, trying to steal what work he had.

By the late 1990s both Nate and Joseph were in their early forties and both had wives and families. They had grown to become much more than simply boss and employee; they had become good friends. They also shared a mutual respect for each other's abilities. Nate understood how important Joseph had been to his success and Joseph was thankful that the years working for Nate had allowed him to build a career in the field of modern manufacturing technology. During the previous ten years, Joseph had risen to the position of factory manager and no longer had as much hands-on activity in the shop, but he enjoyed those few times when he still got to interact with the younger engineers and machine operators.

Each year the Mill Monster seemed to run less and less. When it had mechanical or electrical problems, its replacement parts were hard if not impossible to find. Often Joseph had to reverse engineer the components for the machine and make them on other machines just to keep the old Monster going. Both Nate and Joseph realized the machine should have been scrapped many years earlier, but it was a symbol for both of them. The Mill Monster was the machine that allowed their company to become the success it had become. So they kept it functioning as best as they could for as long as possible.

Then, one day life unfortunately   in a manner as cliché as the subject of a bad country western tune, Joseph came home early from work early one day and found his wife in the act, as they say, with another man.

Insane with rage he immediately went to his dresser drawer and withdrew his gun, which he always kept loaded and ready.

"Joseph! Please. My God! Please don't!" His wife pleaded. The man with whom she shared her bed jumped clumsily from beneath the covers, stark naked, in a last ditch attempt to charge and overpower Joseph. But he never got the chance. With a single blast of gunfire that sounded like a bomb in the close confines of the bedroom, the man's chest exploded in a veritable shower of crimson as he flew back against the far wall from the force of the blast. He seemed to strangely hang motionless in the air for a moment before sliding down along the wall, collapsing to the floor like a tattered rag doll. In his wake was a wide streak of red smeared down the wall.

During the second or so before the man fell, Joseph thought he recognized him. Was it Jim? Jim Erikson? The plumber? he thought. He found it hard to tell with the splatter of gore. He turned to his wife and asked, "Sandy? Really? Jim Erickson? Was that really the best you could do?"

His wife was staring at him as if in a trance, unable to speak coherently, her breath hitching in her chest and coming in short uneven gasps. She was stippled with blood, gore, and fragments of crimson flesh.

"P—pl—please, Joe. Please . . . don't do this! I—I love you, Joe," she somehow managed to stammer.

Joseph just looked down at her and even after her feeble pleas for mercy and her eventual screams of terror he proceeded to fire shot after shot splattering the back wall with her blood and brains.

Next, without a moment's hesitation, Joseph lifted the gun to his head and pulled the trigger, but nothing happened. The pistol had either misfired or was out of bullets. Joseph couldn't recall how many bullets he had fired, nor did he care as his mind was broken and he was beyond all reason.

With no emotion, or remorse, Joseph simply turned and left the room, went downstairs and grabbed several bottles of alcohol from their liquor cabinet and then found a disposable lighter in a drawer in their kitchen. He walked back upstairs then doused the blankets, the corpses, and all the curtains with alcohol while in between taking generous gulps for himself. Once this was done he flicked the lighter to life and set the room ablaze. Then Joseph calmly left the house and headed back to work; the only place he truly felt at home.

The shop was completely empty as it was shut down for the weekend. Being the factory manager, Joseph had his own key. He walked through the dark building, moonlight shining in through the tall windows and roof skylights, slowly making his way back to his favorite machine, his first machine of its kind, the Mill Monster. He powered up the rickety old machine and searched through the tape storage cabinet for the program he wanted. It was a reel of tape labeled with the number O0001. It was the very first program he had ever written for the very first job to run on the machine. Looking back after some twenty or more years Joseph realized it was just a simple single deep-hole drilling program, but at the time, it had seemed as if writing it was an almost insurmountable challenge.

He loaded the Mylar program tape into the machine's ancient mechanical tape reader and pressed the cycle start button. The giant tool changer on the Mill Monster roared as it searched its carousel for the right tool. Joseph knew where the starting point, or origin of the program was in relation to the size of the table, as he had not only written the program but had run the job many times throughout the years.

Then, as he saw the long, two-inch diameter spade drill come into the mill's spindle, he walked up to the machine, hoisted himself up, and leaned backward, lying across its long table and resting the back of his head against its cold cast iron surface. Looking upward through glazed, tear-filled eyes, he saw the steel drill bit rotating rapidly above him in the machine's spindle; at about six hundred revolutions per minute. Joseph could feel the slight table movement as it automatically positioned itself, preparing to carry out its programmed instructions. But instead of getting out the danger zone he simply lay still, staring upward at the large rotating cutting tool.

Next, the Mill Monster did exactly what it did best, what it was programmed to do. It followed the commands of its programmer and brought its tool down toward the table at a rapid feed rate of two hundred inches per minute before slowing down to its programmed feed rate of about two inches per minute. However, before it reached its slowdown point it had already punched its way partially into Joseph's skull, as he knew it would, not quite killing him instantly but rendering him essentially paralyzed, and if he were fortunate enough, brain dead. No one would ever know if he had come to his senses at some point and had realized the mistake he had made, but if so it was far too late for such misgivings.

Then the machine continued its programmed deep hole in and out peck-drilling cycle feeding its way about an inch deeper down into the man's skull before retracting part way out then repeating the process until its final programmed depth was reached. With each peck and retract the spinning tool sprayed a circular area of about twenty feet in diameter with blood and gore as Joseph's body involuntarily thrashed about madly in a unholy dance of death.

That night when the fire department went to Joseph's house to put out the blaze the firemen discovered the charred remnants of Joseph's wife and her lover. At first, they assumed the dead man had been Joseph but one of the volunteer firemen thought he recognized the man as being Jim Erikson, and upon examination of the man's charred wallet contents they confirmed it was him, and not Joseph.

Ashton police chief Max Seiler Jr. soon put together a scenario, which placed Joseph DeNunzio at the top of his suspect list. They searched the house for Joseph's body, assuming a murder-suicide, but did not locate him. Their next thought was that Joseph had fled the scene, skipped town and was now in the wind.

Seiler knew Joseph worked for Nate Bartinski and that they had been good friends for many years so he immediately drove to Nate's home. He hoped Nate might be able to offer some insight into where Joseph might have gone.

"Chief Seiler, there's absolutely no way I can believe Joseph DeNunzio would ever be capable of such an horrendous act," Nate told the police chief. "I just find it impossible to comprehend."

The chief hesitated for a moment then replied, "I know it must be tough for you to consider, Nate, but when a man is emotionally pushed past the brink of reason, anything is possible. The important this is that we find Joseph and at least bring him in for questioning; if for no other reason, then to exclude him from the suspect list. But to be honest with you, it doesn't look very good for him. And so the important question is, Nate . . . where might Joseph have gone?"

"But Max," Nate continued only partially listening to the police chief, "we've both known Joseph for years. Do you really think—" he stopped himself short having finally comprehended what Seiler had just asked and suddenly realizing where Joseph most likely would have gone. "Follow me, Chief," Nate said. "I think if Joseph went anywhere it would be to my factory. It's probably the one place in the world he considers almost like home."

Entering the darkened factory, the group immediately heard the sound of a machine idling, its motors running and emitting an echoing growl, sounding like a wild beast in the otherwise silent cavernous facility. Following the sound they saw the machine's operator light and control panel glowing in the minimal lighting provided by moonlight streaming through the skylights, looking as if it were a museum piece on display. In the center of the macabre tableau they found Joseph's decimated body lying atop the machine table, his arm dangling limply downward, blood dripping from his extended fingers, pooling on the concrete floor in a glistening puddle of crimson gore.

The machine had completed its programmed cycle and had returned to its home position with the tool spindle now stopped, resting high above the table. Staring at the now stationary drill bit Nate saw clumps of hair, torn flesh, and what appeared to be brain matter clinging to the tool as droplets of blood plopped from its tip as if in slow motion falling to the barely recognizable mangled corpse below. Somehow Nate managed to hold back the scream that was desperate to escape his throat, but instead he turned and vomited uncontrollably.

Once the police had removed what was left of the body and finished their investigation, Nate had the machine moved to a dark and seldom used section of the shop and during the next several weeks had it professionally cleaned to remove all traces of that horrible night. The machine sat idle for the entire next year.

Eventually he moved the machine back closer to the manufacturing floor and had tried once again to put the machine into production but each attempt was unsuccessful. Every time he assigned an operator to the machine, that person would inevitably end up getting hurt and often severely injured. One time the result was almost fatal.

During one particular incident a tool holder fell from the spindle while an operator was loading a part and crushed the man's hand, requiring several costly surgeries to repair the damage. In addition there was a workman's compensation claim to deal with and a great deal of lost production time. Another time a high speed rotating tool broke while in the midst of a milling process and flew across the unguarded space, blinding another operator in one eye. Nate's business could not afford too many accidents such as those. In addition, after the first several accidents, superstition began to take over and eventually not a single operator would agree to run the machine. Before long, Nate realized the machine could no longer be used. The risk of injury and potential legal ramifications of running what most considered an unsafe machine were simply cost prohibitive.

Yet for some reason, likely born of sentimentality, Nate could never bring himself to have the machine removed from the factory and scrapped, so he chose instead to move the Mill Monster back to the dark corner of the plant and disconnect all of its electric, hydraulic, and pneumatic lines, leaving it to rust to its present day decrepit state.

Since the tragic death of Joseph DeNunzio and the subsequent injuries caused by the machine, its reputation of living up to its nickname, "Mill Monster," grew to the point of legend and folklore. Stories abounded of reports of mysterious sounds and sightings surrounding the machine, especially on late nights and weekend shifts when the factory was practically empty.

Most of the old-timers, especially those who knew Joseph well, believed the machine was haunted by the dead man's spirit. Many told stories of seeing the transparent ghost of Joseph standing by the machine control as he had done so many years earlier, his glowing white aura shimmering in the moonlight. Others who had heard descriptions of the ghastly condition of Joseph's corpse when it had been found claimed to see his tattered, practically headless body appear lying on the surface of the machine table.

Still others told of times when they had heard strange creaking noises coming from the dark corner where the machine stood, while others claimed to have heard moaning and occasionally screaming. Some went so far as to say they actually saw the machine's spindle turn slowly, despite the fact it had been without power for over twenty years.

Nate knew someday, perhaps when his son, Benjamin, took over the business he might take the initiative to relegate the Mill Monster to the scrap yard where it belonged, but for now it stood as it had done for over forty years; both a symbol of the technology, hard work, and determination, which made Nate's company great, and a tragic reminder of the fragility of life. And perhaps it also offered a suggestion of the possible existence of unknown, unexplainable mysteries, incomprehensible by the minds of men.

What's Wrong With Our House?

The past is never dead. It's not even past.
—William Faulkner, *Requiem for a Nun*

The white-haired woman stood by the window pulling the drapes carefully aside, attempting to sneak a look out into the street. It was October 31st, another Halloween night, and just like every previous Halloween, trick-or-treaters were busy going from house to house in search of the precious goodies they all so desperately desired. But for some strange, unknown reason they seemed to be avoiding her house; almost deliberately so.

"What's wrong with our house?" Gladys Millbury asked of her husband, Harold, who was sitting quietly in his recliner, reading the sports section of the local newspaper and paying little attention to his wife, as was typical of him. The room was clean and tastefully decorated with furnishings they had acquired throughout their forty-three years of marriage.

Harold said, "How the hell should I know, Gladys? Who really knows what goes on inside of the minds of young kids these days? Heaven knows I don't have a clue. But what's the big deal anyway? If they show up, they show up and if they don't, they don't. To be perfectly honest with you, I don't really care if they ever come around. Young kids can often mean nothing but trouble these days. In fact, they're often more trouble than they're worth. Good riddance to bad rubbish as far as I am concerned."

"Oh, Harold," she replied, "that's no way to talk for pity's sake. You sound like such an old fuddy-duddy. It's Halloween night and you know the children in our neighborhood are all good kids. We've always opened our doors to them on Halloween. In the old days we would have been overrun with trick-or-treaters by this time of night. Remember how they always said I gave them the best candy? I was always so proud of that. But now they won't even ring our doorbell anymore. I wonder what happened. It's almost like they seem to be deliberately avoiding us this year. What could possibly be the matter? What in the world do they think is wrong with us?"

"Funny you should ask," Harold replied. "I was starting to wonder what might be wrong with you myself. The way you're standing there staring out into the street. You look like a desperate, starving lost little puppy. For heaven's sake, Gladys, just let it go. So what if the kids choose to ignore us this year? It just means more candy for me."

"Like you can eat all of this candy," Gladys replied looking down into her enormous basket of goodies, "you with your blood sugar issues!"

Gladys and Harold Millbury had been living in the same house at the end of Maple Street for well over thirty years. And for as long as either of them could recall the neighborhood children always flocked to their house for treats faithfully, every Halloween. So Gladys knew something definitely must be amiss to cause them to behave in this fashion.

As Gladys peeked out the front window again she exclaimed, "Oh my goodness, Harold! You should see this! Several of the kids just crossed over to the other side of the street as if they were making a point of avoiding our house. I even saw a couple of them looking back then quickly looked away. They seemed to have looks of terror on their faces. It was like they were afraid to come here or something. Why would anyone be afraid to come here, Harold? We're good people. What's wrong with these kids?"

Harold decided to go back to ignoring his wife and continue to read his newspaper.

Outside, the neighborhood kids who Gladys had seen from the window were doing exactly as she had described, walking across the street, pushing and shoving each other playfully, occasionally giving wary glances back toward the house. Every so often one of the kids would point back toward their house then make spooky gestures with his hands at the younger children and laugh hysterically. The small children would look back at the house quickly before hurrying to be back with the group.

The house sat in darkness, illuminated only by the pale moonlight shining through the branches of the tall oak trees in the overgrown front yard. The trees had lost their leaves a month earlier and now stood like colossal multi-limbed monstrous sentries guarding the mysterious home with its battered, paint-chipped facade and foot-high weeds surrounding the broken brick walkway.

The neighborhood children all knew about the Millbury place and they had all heard the many frightening stories surrounding the house. They knew both the real history of the property, which was in itself terrifying enough, but they also knew all of the local legends and those were certainly enough to keep even the most daring of them away.

As the true story of the house went, a nice elderly retired couple named Gladys and Harold Millbury had once owned the home. Mr. Millbury had been retired from the railroad and Mrs. Millbury had worked her entire career as a nurse at a local hospital. Every Halloween children from all over would flock to the Millbury place since Gladys was reputed to give the best candy in town.

There was also a false reputation that followed the Millburys. Since the couple had no children, lived frugally, and both had generous pensions, it was assumed they were quite well off financially. This was completely untrue. The two weren't starving by any means and Gladys was quite generous with her precious trick-or-treaters, but the couple was far from wealthy. Unfortunately, those particular false stories about them being rich had reached the ears of some local undesirables and the result was a horrific crime the likes of which the small town had never seen before or since.

Twelve years earlier to the day, October 31st, Halloween night, the couple had opened their home to trick-or-treaters as they had done for so many years before. Gladys waited by the window with her bowl of candy, watching for children, while Harold sat in his recliner reading the sports section as always. It had been a very successful evening with many children enjoying their treats.

However, later that night while the couple slept, persons unknown broke into the house, murdered the couple in their sleep then robbed the house of whatever they could find. The place had been ransacked as if the killers had been looking for caches of hidden money. But of course there was no treasure to be found.

And there was much more to the story than just two people being murdered in their sleep. Word had leaked that the murderers had conducted some sort of strange, bizarre and possibly satanic rituals with the bodies. It was said the twisted perpetrators had savagely dismembered the couple's bodies and had arranged the parts in a bizarre manner. Witnesses said the scene resembled something which might be described as a modern art show in Hell. This included limbs from Harold's body being attached to Gladys' torso and vice versa.

It was said that Gladys' breasts had been hacked off and attached to Harold's chest. Likewise Harold's genitals were severed and placed between Gladys' legs. Their stomachs had been sliced open and the room decorated with their bloody intestines like some unimaginable pink and crimson garland. Both of their heads had been decapitated and placed atop their dresser, as if posed to witness the hideous tableau being staged before them. The room stank like the inside of a slaughter house, which was exactly what it had become.

The unholy display of mangled and reordered body parts was so horrifying and beyond anyone's ability to understand, that every investigator on the scene was unable to keep from vomiting. Perhaps the most disturbing part of it all was the writing on the wall behind the bed, as if the killers had wanted to come up with a title for the macabre scene. Written crudely with hands dipped in the couple's blood were the words "Happy Halloween."The criminals were never caught.

If there was any consolation to be taken from the scene of unimaginable butchery was the county coroner's report suggested the couple had likely been killed instantly and did not have to suffer. He even suggested they had probably died so quickly that they might have not even known what had happened to them.

So, from the coroner's single statement the legends began, spread and grew as such legends often did. Stories of late night sightings of Gladys standing, looking out of the front window abounded. And this was especially prevalent on Halloween night, the anniversary of the murders, when it was believed she still stood watching for her beloved trick-or-treaters. There were also tales of the two headless specters being seen floating inside the home.

Because of the savagery of the murders committed in the house, no one would dare buy it. As a result it soon fell to disrepair and eventually to ruin. And now every year the neighborhood children would make it a point to cross the street on Halloween night in order to stay as far from the Millbury house as possible.

"I just don't get it." Gladys said as she looked out of her living room window, "They are avoiding us like we have the plague or something. I can't figure it out, Harold. Our house used to be a magnet for children at Halloween, but no longer. What's wrong with our house?"

"Forget it," Harold said. "Look. This is all pointless. I'm tired anyway. I think I'll head up to bed for the night. "

So, Harold stood and set the newspaper down on the end table and went up the stairs to bed. The date of the paper read October 31st but the year was not the current year; it was twelve years earlier. He read the exact same paper every October 31st. And this was the same scenario, which he and Gladys had played out every Halloween night since the horrific event had occurred. But to them, it was always be the first time, always new, always fresh, and it would be eternal.

Grundies

*Adapt or perish, now as ever, is nature's inexorable
imperative.*
—H. G. Wells

Nature does not hurry, yet everything is accomplished.
—Lao Tzu

Chad looked out through the windshield onto the dark
slick expanse of highway ahead of him and suddenly
realized he had absolutely no idea where he was. Up ahead
a road sign reflected in his headlights through the fog and
misty rain, becoming more visible the closer he got. The
sign read "Erie 50 MI." Chad was suddenly perplexed.

The last road sign he had remembered seeing had
indicated that he still had eighty miles to travel. And now
this sign said only fifty miles. He wondered if the previous
sign had been wrong or perhaps he might have read it
incorrectly. But he was almost certain the sign had said
eighty miles. If he were right, then it meant that for the
past thirty miles or roughly forty minutes, he had been
essentially driving on autopilot, completely oblivious to his
surroundings. Chad looked at the clock on the dashboard
display and confirmed that forty-five minutes had actually
passed.

He was not completely surprised by such a concept,
since Chad was quite certain that at one time or another
everyone found themselves driving on autopilot. He
assumed nothing had happened of any note worthiness or
most certainly he would have snapped out of his trance; at
least he hoped that would be the case.

He remembered having experienced similar events on
several occasion in the past. But this was the first time in
his many years behind the wheel that he had zoned out so
extremely as to not be able to recall one single detail of the

past three quarters of an hour. He was beside himself with confusion.

Chad supposed it was his own fault. Usually when he drove from eastern Pennsylvania to the far northwest side of the state he traveled via the turnpike, taking it past Pittsburgh, almost to the Ohio border before heading north toward Erie. This route took him on all main highways, most of which were set up to accommodate four lanes of traffic or better.

That particular route was longer in terms of miles traveled as it formed the left and bottom sides of a right triangle. However, with the higher speed limits those expressways offered with such an open roadway it often made the trip go quickly; however it was also an extremely boring driving experience. Chad would often listen to audio books to help him deal with the monotony, but sometimes it just got to be too much for him.

For that reason, Chad had chosen not to take the turnpike on this trip. He had instead gotten the not-so-ingenious idea that it might be more interesting to get off the turnpike after Somerset and head northwest along the hypotenuse of the triangle, thereby taking the theoretically shortest route to Erie. At the time it made perfect sense to him because everyone knows the shortest distance between two points is a straight line. But although it may have been shorter in terms of miles traveled, the trip ended up being much longer in terms of hours spent on the highway.

Unlike the turnpike, most of the roads Chad took along the scenic route were country two-lanes, which wound through rural areas, small towns, and vast forestlands. He couldn't recall how long it had been since he had seen a familiar fast food restaurant. There were few if any gas stations along the route either and those he did see appeared to be of the Mom and Pop variety; looking frighteningly like those run-down shacks often depicted in horror movies about deranged hillbillies. He suddenly had a flashback to a scene from the 1970s movie *Deliverance*, which caused his stomach to tighten just a bit.

Chad recalled with displeasure how just before he zoned out he had stopped at a local combination gas station and general store. It was the sort of place that kept fish bait in the same cooler as popsicles. He remembered the deplorable condition of the store with peeling paint on its exterior and the well-worn dusty wood plank flooring inside. The place had a dank and musty smell common to such old buildings.

And the old man working behind the service counter was equally as disheveled in appearance. That character had been a scrawny old coot in a stained and yellowed wife-beater, wearing a soiled camouflaged trucker's cap with a brim blackened from filthy finger smudges. The old-timer looked as though he had not showered for days nor had he shaved for weeks, apparent by the grizzled stubble which covered his face in irregular patches.

Across the room from the service counter an odd looking overweight young man, perhaps thirty-five, was precariously perched on a rocking chair and staring slack-jawed at Chad who stood sopping wet, dripping water onto the aged plank floor. When Chad first walked into the store the rocker had been in motion but it stopped as soon as he approached the counter.

It was apparent to Chad from the odd man's demeanor he was a dullard, perhaps mentally retarded. Although Chad knew both of those terms were considered politically incorrect, they seemed to fit that particular individual. Chad thought to himself in words that would be considered even less socially acceptable, What a bunch of inbred mutants. This idea solidified Chad's earlier *Deliverance* impression even further in his mind, which made him feel very uncomfortable. He recalled how that single movie had bothered him in ways no other movie had ever done before or since.

But despite his many misgivings and his discomfort with the place, Chad completed his transaction without incident. He could not however, seem to shake the unusual sensation slithering down his spine as he walked out of the store. Even though he didn't bother to look back, Chad was certain both the owner and his subhuman associate, perhaps the man's own offspring, were still staring at him. He could almost feel their eyes boring holes in his back. Chad had climbed uneasily behind the wheel then quickly drove away, deciding not to stop anywhere again until he saw some signs of real, honest-to-goodness civilization.

For Chad, the word 'civilization' meant areas of the state with familiar places like McDonalds, Burger King, Wendy's, Pizza Hut or any of the other national franchises, which he knew he could usually count on to be clean and have a staff of cordial, friendly workers. Those were the sorts of places that would ensure him he had truly left the untamed wilderness and had safely made it back to at least some semblance of normalcy. That is to say some place much less bizarre than and much more socially acceptable than what he thought of as Clem and Bubba's Inbred Emporium.

Chad usually didn't consider himself a snob, a bigot, or a prejudiced type of person. But the more he thought about it the more he realized most of those types of people likely seldom thought of themselves as such. So unfortunately, maybe he was more of a bigot then he realized. This made him feel momentarily guilty for having had such negative feelings toward the odd pair in the gas station. He really didn't know the two people and as such had no business prejudging them. But when he recalled how all of his internal alarms had seemed to go off at once in their presence, he decided perhaps his displeasure was not necessarily the result of bigotry but was some natural built-in early warning system.

He had driven away from the store as quickly as possible, perhaps a bit over the posted speed limit, extremely anxious about putting as much distance between himself and the strange pair. He had started to imagine a scenario picturing the two weird characters leaving the store, climbing into a beat-up rusted Ford pickup truck, and speeding after him with the intention of forcing him off the highway, taking him prisoner and doing whatever those sorts of creepy people did whenever they kidnapped someone. Once again he recalled *Deliverance* and the scene where the character played by Ned Beatty was being raped by a group of mountain psychos. Another cold chill ran down his back as he repeatedly took quick glances into his rearview mirror to make sure he was not being followed and was still alone; which, fortunately, he was.

He remembered looking up at the wet roadway and saw a sign stating "Erie 80 MI" and he had breathed a sigh of relief. He knew he would arrive at his destination in less than two hours and he hoped to find more signs of civilization long before then. But that had been the very last thing Chad could recall. One minute he had been driving along the rainy roadway replaying the strange scene from the gas station, then everything went blank until he found himself passing the sign proclaiming Erie was now only fifty miles away. He had no idea what had happened to the last thirty miles; more than forty minutes of travel.

Shortly after passing the most recent road sign he entered another heavily forested area with trees towering so high and thick over the roadway as to create a blanket of shade so dark it was almost like night. The rain did not seem to fall heavily under the canopy of greenery but dripped steadily. The misty fog was just as dense as ever. Chad, once again, could feel himself starting to zone out and he tried turning on the radio to help him stay alert, but all he got was static.

He fiddled with the tuning button for a few second more before finally giving up. When he looked up from the radio he was suddenly startled. Something; a creature of some sort, possibly a dog or cat scurried out from the underbrush and ran directly into the path of his car. Chad swerved in a desperate attempt to avoid hitting whatever it was and almost overcompensated, which might have resulted in his crashing the car into a tree. When he swerved to avoid the creature, Chad succeeded in missing the thing with his right front tire. But then he felt a thud under his car on the left side as he realized he had unfortunately struck the creature with his left rear tire. He also heard the animal let out a high-pitched screech and then he knew for certain he had hit it.

Chad pulled over onto the sparse shoulder of the highway and sat breathing rapidly as he looked into his rearview mirror. With the minimal light coming through the canopy of trees he could see whatever it was he had

struck lying near the middle of the road just on his side of
the double yellow line. And it appeared to still be moving.

"Oh man!" Chad exclaimed with frustration, realizing
he was now faced with the decision of whether to just drive
off or to go back and see how bad things really were. He
had hit and killed animals on highways before, small
rabbits or squirrels that had wandered onto the road, and
in every case he had simply driven away. But each of those
times he had actually seen the type of animal he had hit.
This time he had not.

Although he could tell it was fairly large he could not
say for certain whether it was a wild animal or if perhaps it
was someone's pet. He recalled passing a number of rural
mailboxes along the road and it was entirely possible that
someone's dog or cat had strayed onto the highway. Chad
hated when people accidently ran over pets then fled the
scene. It seemed so wrong to him; and for a very good
reason.

When he had been a very young boy, perhaps five or
six, he had a pet beagle named "Rascal." That dog had
been struck and killed by a car, but the driver never
stopped to tell anyone; he had just driven away. Chad had
been out playing with his friend when they came upon the
ravaged remains of his once beloved pet. Young Chad had
no idea who had killed his dog, but he wished the man had
not just driven away leaving Rascal unattended. He often
wondered if his dog might have just been badly hurt and
not killed immediately. Maybe his pet could have been
helped and perhaps didn't have to die. But he would never
know for certain.

Reluctantly, Chad slowly opened the door to his car
and placed his left foot on the roadway. As he did so, he
caught another reflection in the side mirror and between
the patches of fog he could see the creature moving slightly
once again. Apparently, he had not killed it but perhaps
only stunned it. In the darkness of the shadowed and
misty highway, he was still unable to identify what type of
animal it was. Although he was quite concerned about the
creature, he was also equally uncomfortable with the idea
of approaching the unknown thing to render assistance.
Yet he understood he couldn't just drive away and leave it

where it was. He was certain eventually another car or truck would come by and hit it again, possibly finishing it off.

If he got to the creature in time it might be still alive and there might be a chance for him to do something to help it survive. He reached into his pocket and checked his phone, only to see there was no cell service available. He thought again about getting back into the car and driving away then recalled how badly he had felt as a child upon finding his own dog dead along a highway. The rain apparently had picked up because now even under the trees there was a steady drizzle.

He stood next to his car and after a brief hesitation he drummed up the courage to cautiously walk up the road toward the injured animal. As he got closer, Chad heard a rustling in the underbrush along the side of the road and momentarily was startled, wondering if some other animal, perhaps a wild one, might be lurking in the underbrush. Perhaps it was a predator or a scavenger eager to take advantage of the wounded animal.

Then Chad thought he saw the bushes moving in several spots along the highway as if some small unseen creatures were scurrying about just out of sight. Once again he considered running back to his car, jumping inside, and driving away no matter how much he felt obliged to stay, but once again he realized he could not. He looked at his watch, realizing he was now most definitely going to be late for his appointment in Erie and would likely have to reschedule it until later in the day.

He shook his head with frustration and walked toward the quivering mass of fur lying in the middle of the roadway. As he got closer he heard it make a low guttural growl as the thing began to raise itself upright to the best of its limited ability. To his surprise, it was not a dog or cat or any sort of family pet. The creature he had struck was a large groundhog.

Chad suddenly had a memory from his childhood about how his father used to call groundhogs "whistle pigs" because of the way the male groundhogs would stand on their hind legs and utter a whistling sound to attract the attention of females. He was told they also issued the whistling sound to warn other groundhogs of impending danger. Although Chad had never seen or heard such a display he assumed they must do something like that or else his father would never have referred to them as such. He had forgotten the term until that very moment as he saw the thing trying to stand upright.

Then another name suddenly popped into his mind; "grundie." His wife and several of their Berks County friends referred to groundhogs as grundies. Not being a native of that area of Pennsylvania as his wife had been, he assumed it to be a local colloquialism.

"A grundie!" Chad said aloud. "Now what in the hell am I supposed to do?" He knew groundhogs were herbivores and as such didn't eat meat but that didn't mean it wouldn't attack him if it felt threatened. Meat-eater or not it still had teeth and claws.

He had originally been concerned about dealing with a wounded pet, but now that he knew the creature was a wild, feral animal he was even more unsure of how or if he should go about approaching the thing. Then he heard the creature moan a mournful cry in a way that could only be the result of intense pain.

Chad carefully walked around the creature trying to get a better view of it to determine the extent of its injuries. He was quite certain it could not crawl away or surely it would have done so already. Then as he crossed over to the opposite side of the double yellow line his stomach clenched with revulsion at the sight before him.

The back third of the poor creature was completely decimated, having been squashed flat by Chad's tire while the remaining two thirds of the creature writhed in agony. The groundhog's back legs were no longer recognizable, having become part of the shattered jumble of fur, blood and, entrails smeared along the centerline of the highway.

The upper part of the creature's body was vertical as the thing thrashed about slashing with its clawed forepaws while hissing and growling and snapping its jaws savagely as if even in the throes of eminent death it was still trying to fight off its human adversary. It issued a high-pitched whistling noise so loud it hurt Chad's ears. Then he heard a series of similar whistling noises coming from the rustling underbrush.

Chad found himself wracked with conflicting emotions; pity for the poor dying groundhog, guilt for being the one responsible for its pain, fear that he might end up scratched or bitten himself, knowledge that he would remember this unspeakable nightmare for as long as he lived, and an understanding of what he had to do next.

He could tell by the level of damage his car had done that the creature was as good as dead. The thing was obviously suffering with unimaginable pain and the only right thing for him to do was to somehow put the pathetic creature out of its misery, and to do so as quickly as possible. But how could he?

For a moment, Chad considered perhaps backing his car over top of the creature and finishing it off but the idea of the additional mess it might make on his undercarriage revolted him. What could he do? Then he had an idea; not the best of solutions, but one he believed to be a workable plan.

If he could just find a large rock, he could sneak up on the creature from behind and bash in its skull, killing it quickly and humanely while keeping himself out of harm's way in the process. Chad was fairly certain with its squashed lower body stuck fast to the highway the creature would not be able to turn around to attempt to attack him when he got close enough.

He slowly walked back to the side of the roadway to try to find a rock of sufficient size to do what had to be done. As he did so, the creature continued growling, hissing, and whistling until Chad passed beyond its field of vision. Then the animal went back down into a crouched position where it began pathetically licking its bleeding wounds.

Since there was little light under the dense trees Chad had to squint in the darkness to try to find what he needed. The rain trickling down his face and into his eyes made the chore even more difficult. There was no doubt the wretched groundhog was beyond healing, but Chad had no idea where he would find the necessary courage to actually put the creature down in such an up close and intimate fashion. He suddenly felt like a murderer planning a crime.

As he searched for the proper size rock along the side of the road, Chad once again heard the rustling in the undergrowth. He did is best not to let the strange sounds unnerve him as his groping hands finally found what they were looking for. Chad pulled hard on the stone, wrestling it from the damp muddy soil. His hair was now flattened to his head and rain streamed down his face. Chad shook his head to try to shoo away the water droplets. His clothing was likewise sodden.

He lifted the large rock, carefully holding it on an area that was free of mud and debris in order to maintain a sufficient grip. Chad believed the stone was heavy enough to accomplish the task at hand but it was unfortunately not quite as smooth as he hoped. It had numerous sharp outcroppings which he realized might make the job a bit messier than he would have originally preferred. He began to walk slowly back toward the mortally wounded creature, which was plastered to the middle of the road. As he did so he tried to steel himself for what was to come next.

As Chad got closer, the creature apparently sensed his approach from behind and sat up once again whistling while making a futile attempt to turn its body to see what was approaching from his blind spot. Chad lifted the heavy rock high above his own head then brought it down hard upon the wounded creature's skull. He heard a sharp cracking sound as simultaneously, some foul-smelling liquid, likely blood and brain matter, shot from the thing's head, flew in his direction and coated his shirt, pants, face, and hands with a disgusting, musky-smelling stench.

His stomach turned over not only from the vile smell but the idea of the nature of the substance that was now was all over him. He turned his head and vomited on the highway. The animal fell to the roadway as Chad dropped the deadly stone and it rolled a few feet away from the creature's corpse landing next to the steaming puddle of vomit.

Chad was bent over waiting for his uncontrollable retching to stop. After it finally did, he stood for a moment taking in the horror before him. The grundie was most certainly dead; its ruined body was now just a mass of glistening unrecognizable fur. He had actually killed it although he could scarcely believe it himself. Chad knew if he returned to this same spot in a few days, after the scavengers had done their best to decimate the corpse and numerous other vehicles had run over the remains, there would be nothing left but a flattened mass.

"Road pizza" is what he had often jokingly called such a sight. He had seen such similar creatures squashed flat countless times before. Whenever he and his wife were driving and saw such an unidentifiable furry pancake along a road they often simply referred to it as "a dead"; as in a dead skunk or a dead raccoon or a dead groundhog. But since it was no longer identifiable, they just called it "a dead." And what he now saw on the highway definitely fit into that particular category. At those previous times when he had said "a dead" it had seemed funny in the darkest of senses. But now nothing about what he saw seemed in any way funny to him.

He picked up the large rock and turned to return it to its original location as there was no point in having some other car strike the stone and blow out a tire or perhaps cause an accident. As he did so he heard a chorus of wild hissing, chittering, and whistling coming from the woods beyond. He also thought he saw many sets of glowing eye staring at him from the underbrush.

Grundies! He thought, realizing that the now dead creature likely had been part of a larger community and perhaps even had left baby groundhogs behind. Seething with anger and frustration at the unpleasant situation he had found himself forced into, Chad hurled the boulder with all of his strength in the direction of the woods secretly hoping to hear one of the things screech in pain as the stone found its mark; although all he heard was the creatures scattering with fear it gave him a great deal of satisfaction.

Chad was no longer feeling quite like himself; at least not the man he thought he was. The events of the day made him feel very different; as if he had earned his rightful place at the top of the food chain. Despite his earlier reservations, Chad now felt some deeply hidden recessive and primal rush of adrenalin, which he assumed primitive man must have felt when hunting for his food.

He could smell his own sweat mixed with the raw, woodsy stench from the felled creature and it made him feel savage and alive in a way he had never felt before. His breathing was deep and seemed to echo in the now silent woods. Then the rush faded quickly and Chad's momentary emotions of being master of all he surveyed likewise began to dissipate.

Now he suddenly realized he was transforming back to being just regular white-collar Chad standing in the middle of a highway with stinking groundhog gunk all over him, wild-eyed like a madman panting and sweating like a rutting hog. Although he still felt the slight remnants of the previous euphoria, he was rapidly coming back to reality.

His mind now returning to its proper perspective, Chad realized that as soon as he could find a cell phone signal he was going to have to reschedule his meeting, likely changing it until the following morning. After the trying day he had experienced so far, Chad was certain he would need to find a roadside rest stop or somewhere to clean up to the best of his ability and then find a hotel to crash for the night.

He planned on taking the longest and hottest shower he had ever taken in his life and then would find a way to dump all of his soiled clothing in a trashcan or dumpster somewhere. He had no intention of taking them home for his wife to wash; not with all the grundie gunk on them. Next he planned on finding a bar and drinking very heavily before heading back to his room and collapsing early into bed. A good night's sleep would be just what he needed to make all of the badness of the day go by the wayside. And now, as his adrenalin rush diminished, his strength seemed to wane right along with it.

In the distance he saw his car, the front door still standing open and the interior light illuminated. The car couldn't have been more than thirty feet away but in his exhausted condition, the slow trudge back felt as if Chad had been walking for miles. The day's events were definitely taking their toll and Chad could feel himself mentally and physically crashing rapidly.

When he reached his car, he literally fell behind the wheel and it took all of his strength to fasten his seatbelt and pull the driver's door closed. Once inside the close confines of the car Chad was immediately aware of just how rank he smelled. He started the engine and put down all of the windows. He felt as if he might start vomiting all over again. Chad hoped once he got moving and the wind began whipping through the windows it might blow the worst of the smell away.

"Woo baby I really stink!" Chad said aloud with an unexpected chuckle as the stress finally began to leave him, quickly and surprisingly replaced by an insane sense of glee. In fact, he was so relieved that he began to feel almost giddy. "I guess it's a good thing I'm not near Punxsutawney or else old Groundhog Phil might have seen his last shadow today." Then he began to laugh madly as tears of relief streamed down his soiled face. That was the exact moment when he felt the first lightning bolt of pain as a tiny pair of teeth sunk deeply into the back of his neck.

Chad tried to reach back and fight off whatever it was that was gnawing on his flesh but could not reach the thing. Then he heard a chorus of whistling which sounded less like a warning cry and more like a war cry. He then felt dozens of other sets of tiny teeth chewing away at him in various places; his face, arms, legs, and his throat. He screamed and thrashed about madly trying desperately to free himself from the bonds of his safety belt while he could feel himself being literally eaten alive. Amid his wilt convulsions of agony blood flew wildly splattering the car's interior and windshield with gore.

The last thing Chad ever saw were two tiny angry red eyes staring into his own eyes from the heavy, furry thing that had perched atop his head as it bent over showing him its yellowed teeth, which popped one of his eyeballs like a grape. Groundhogs might traditionally be herbivores by nature but for at least one moment in time these particular grundies had changed their ways in order to partake in a very special feast of vengeance.

The Shutter

To say Eddie Johnson loved craft shows would be incorrect; the truth was, at best, Eddie tolerated them. His wife, Maxine, however, adored the events. In an attempt to be a good husband, Eddie made a point of accompanying his wife to every craft show or fair she chose to attend.

There was one obstacle Eddie had to overcome however, and that was the simple fact that he had absolutely no interest whatsoever in anything having to do with crafts. So he found a way to tolerate them, and his solution was food.

Early on, Eddie found one similar thing about every craft-type event; they all sold some of the best junk food in the world, and it didn't matter what time of day either. If they attended a show in the early morning, there were always plenty of vendors selling every type of unhealthy breakfast food imaginable—pancakes, eggs, sausage, bacon, hash brown potatoes, home fries, you name it— most of which was dripping with butter.

If they arrived at or after noon, he would find steak sandwiches, sausage sandwiches, ice cream, funnel cakes, soft pretzels, and other such normally frowned upon delicacies. For Eddie, it was like finding an oasis in the middle of hell.

Maxine would wander from table to table examining the various handmade items while Eddie followed in her wake dripping ice cream, slurping a soda, wiping sauce off of his shirt or powdered sugar out of his beard. As long as Maxine was happy and Eddie was fed, everything else would take care of itself.

After several years, and many pounds later, they happened to find themselves on one particular Saturday at a new craft show about two hours from their home. It was the first time the community had scheduled the event and judging by the successful turnout of both artisans and customers, it would likely become an annual show.

There were literally hundreds of craft stands set up with their pop up canopies, folding tables, and makeshift shelving, each holding countless treasures waiting to be purchased. Many of the vendors had handheld satellite credit card machines, allowing them to process cards on the spot. One vendor was having trouble with reception and had to stand on a chair every time he had to make a transaction, but Eddie assumed it must still be better than the old credit card imprint swiping method.

The particular types of crafts Maxine especially liked were those made from old used wood products that had been cleaned up a bit and painted with some country design; the more rustic and primitive the better. She especially liked those types of items that could be hung on the wall rather than those that took up floor space.

Their house was adorned with a variety of former cabinet doors, window panes, desktops, wooden ironing boards, and other such common items. These things had found new lives in the hands of the artists who had probably picked up the items for next to nothing, painted various country images and scenes on them, then slapped on a fifty or hundred dollar price tag, to be sold to people such as Maxine and Eddie. Eddie usually didn't mind the cost and for the most part paid little attention to the items Maxine purchased, as home décor was not his forte.

"Look, Eddie!" Maxine shouted with the boisterous giggling glee of a schoolgirl. "Isn't it great?" she cried. "It will look perfect in the first floor hall, just outside your study."

Eddie looked at the item in question, doing his best to seem excited while thinking about how great an ice cream sandwich would go down right about now. "Yeah. It looks fine to me," he replied. The fact was, it did not look fine at all. It actually looked like a worthless piece of junk to Eddie.

The "work of art" was an old wooden window shutter, consisting of three pieces of wood perhaps six inches wide and five feet long, connected by iron cross pieces. The thing still had its rusted hinges attached, he supposed for authenticity or some such thing. It was grayed and weathered from years of exposure to the elements, and it seemed to have been scorched or burned at one time.

The craftswoman, who created the piece—for some reason they always called the worst junk "pieces"— explained how she coated the entire shutter with many layers of shellac to seal in its original "essence" and eliminate the charred wood smells.

Eddie found the woman rather odd and Bohemian in her appearance, but he often found many such vendors to be strange. Next the woman explained how she then painted her artwork on the shellacked surface. To Eddie, it looked like just another boring country-fied scene, consisting of a tall, elongated, brightly-colored rooster with a farm scene behind him including a rustic split rail fence, a barn, some hay, and several little chickens running about.

Maxine was giddy with excitement. "Eddie, you won't believe the deal I am getting," she whispered conspiratorially. "This piece usually sells for one hundred and fifty dollars, but we can have it for half price." Eddie thought seventy-five dollars was about seventy-three dollars more than he would have paid for it but hid his displeasure and handed over his credit card.

After the transaction was complete, Maxine suggested, "Honey? Why don't you take this out to the van so you don't have to carry it around all day, and I will meet you at that booth over there."

All of the stands looked the same to Eddie, but then he saw a landmark he actually could recognize near the approximate area where Maxine was pointing. "You mean the one next to the caramel popcorn stand?"

"Yes, that's the one," she replied. "I will meet you then after you drop off the artwork."

"No problemo," Eddie said and proceeded toward the parking lot, wondering how such nonsense could be considered artwork. By the time he got all the way back to the van, the shutter had started to become quite heavy. He opened the hatch of the van and laid the shutter in the area reserved for their newfound treasures.

He was busy thinking about munching on a nice bag of caramel popcorn when he causally glanced at the shutter and thought he noticed some strange image forming in the background, between two rungs of a split rail fence. It was a horrible scarred face of a man, whose eyes seemed to be wild with insanity. When he blinked, the image was gone. "What the Hell!" Eddie said and looked again at the shutter, but no matter how he cocked his head, he could not get the image to reappear.

On his way back to meet Maxine he walked by the stand where they purchased the shutter and saw the woman watching the crowd for another potential customer. He decided to inquire a bit more about the mysterious artwork.

"Excuse me," Eddie asked the artist. "That shutter we just bought—"

"Oh yes," she replied enthusiastically. "It was one of my favorite works."

"Uh, yes." He said. "That was really . . . something. I was wondering, do you know where that shutter came from? I mean . . . originally?"

The woman seemed to be thinking for a while then said somewhat reluctantly, "You know, I am not quite certain. You see. My husband buys all of the items I paint from a variety of sources, such as yard sales, auctions, fire sales and such."

"It is very important to me that I learn more about the origin of the shutter," Eddie said, noticing a strange look appear on the woman's face. He quickly made up a lie saying, "When people come to our home and look at our wall hangings, they all want to know about the artist and how to get in touch with them. They often also ask about the origin of the piece of furniture the artist chose to paint. I suppose it gives them a better feel for the work or something. Is there any possible way your husband might recall where he bought the shutters?"

The woman now seemed more at ease. "Why don't I ask him when I get home, and if you are still interested, you can give me a call or email me? I will be happy to let you know what I find out." She reached down and picked up one of her business cards, handing it to Eddie, who tucked it into his jacket pocket.

Then he said to the woman, "Thank you very much. I will get in touch with you in a few days and see what you have found out." Eddie had never gotten so deeply involved in Maxine's purchases before; then again, none of her prior purchases had managed to scare the daylights out of him either.

Once they arrived back home, Maxine began carrying each piece from room to room deciding where it would look best. After several hours of work, placing hangers on the walls with Maxine supervising to assure the locations were correct, all of the newly purchased items were in place, and Eddie was ready for dinner.

After dinner Eddie retired to his study to work on paying some bills. Looking up from his desk he saw the shutter hanging outside in the hall. He had a direct view of the strange thing from his desk. He tried ignoring it, but the more he tried the more he seemed to want to stare at it. Frustrated, he got up, went over and closed the door to his study blocking the view.

When he was just about finished, he thought he heard what sounded like someone laughing. It was not a happy laugh but one sounding maniacal, like the laughter of a crazy man. He got up from his desk and quickly opened the door to his study to see if he could pinpoint the source of the laughter. But as soon as the door was opened, the laughter stopped. Eddie shook his head, deciding it was time to pack it in for the day, as he was obviously exhausted.

He went to the family room and joined Maxine for some evening television before going to bed. He no sooner sat down in his recliner than he was fast asleep. Next thing he knew, Maxine shook him out of a sound sleep appearing frightened. It took him a moment or two to get reoriented with his surroundings and asked, "What's wrong Maxine?"

"Eddie. Do you smell that?" she asked.

Eddie took a moment to sniff the air then replied, "Yes, I think I smell smoke." He jumped from his chair as Maxine followed him down the hall toward his office, which seemed to be the source of the smell. Inside, he found the contents of his trashcan ablaze. Without thinking, he opened the French doors leading out to their patio from the office, and grabbed the trashcan, throwing it out the door and landing it square in the middle of their swimming pool.

"What happened, Eddie?" she asked. "What were you doing in here that could have caused the fire? You weren't smoking again were you?"

Eddie had quit smoking about ten years earlier and had, on occasion, had relapsed during that time. "Absolutely not!" Eddie insisted. "I don't have any cigarettes anywhere in the house, and I don't keep lighters or matches in the office either."

"Well, something must have started it!" Maxine said with an accusatory tone. "It certainly didn't start by itself. Just make sure everything else is secure around here, and then come to bed. I've had enough excitement for today." With that, she left of the office, pulling the study door closed behind her.

Eddie stood scratching his head. He was certain there was nothing he could have possibly done that would have caused a fire to ignite, but obviously something had caused it. He closed the French doors to the patio, watching the smoldering trashcan glowing in the night as it slowly sunk down into the pool. "Just great!" Eddie thought. "One more job for me to do tomorrow . . . clean the stupid swimming pool."

Then Eddie heard it again, the strange maniacal laughter coming from somewhere out in the hall. He threw the door to his study open, but the laughter immediately stopped. He looked across the hall at the shutter, certain he would once again see the hideous image emerge from the background, but it did not. Then, shaking his head to clear his mind, Eddie closed the door to his office and went to bed.

Over the course of the next several days Eddie and Maxine continued to find strange mini-fires throughout the house. The day after the trashcan fire, Eddie had gone around the house changing the batteries in each of the smoke detectors since they had obviously failed to warn them about the office fire. Now with fresh batteries, as soon as any smoke was detected the alarms sounded.

One day they had found a scented decorative candle knocked over on its side, which had set fire to a lace doily. That fire was blamed on the cat, Mr. Kitty, who they assumed must have overturned the candle. Another time they smelled gas and found one of the burners on their kitchen gas stove had been left turned on. That instance they blamed on a "senior moment," being cautious not to point the finger of blame at each other. There were other such near misses throughout the week, and there were also several times when both Eddie and Maxine thought they heard strange laughter throughout the house.

On Thursday Eddie noticed Mr. Kitty sitting in the hall outside of the study staring at the shutter hanging on the wall. The cat was growling low and deep in the back of his throat, something he rarely did. Shortly thereafter, the cat was nowhere to be found. Eddie had suspected he may have gotten outside and was roaming the neighborhood. That was, until Saturday morning when he found the cat's charred and burned carcass lying in the bushes next to his office patio door. He disposed of the cat but never said anything to Maxine, assuming it was better if she thought the cat had run away than to know of its horrible demise.

Eddie realized there was something about the shutter, that one particular work. All of the problems they were experiencing started happening after bringing the shutter into the house. Eddie went to the hall closet and reached into his jacket pocket, retrieving one of the business cards from the woman at the craft show.

He walked outside and using his cell phone dialed the number. The woman answered on the second ring. He introduced himself and asked what she had found out about the shutter they had bought.

"Yes. Well . . ." she said hesitantly, "George, my husband, luckily remembered exactly where he bought the shutter. In fact, he bought about thirty exactly like it at the same time. He was traveling through Virginia and saw a sign for a fire sale. It was a place called the Shady Rest just outside of Fredericksburg. I think it was some sort of convalescent center or something like that that had burned down during a tragic fire. I hope the information is helpful.

And I hope everything is OK, and you are happy with the work."

"Ah, yes . . ." Eddie said absently. "Everything is fine. As I said, I was simply curious. Thank you very much."

Eddie hung up the phone and then walked to his office, being careful as he walked past the shutter to act as nonchalant as possible. He felt a bit foolish behaving this way, but there were just so many strange and dangerous events taking place during the past week, he could not take any chances.

When he got to his office, he closed the door and immediately logged into his computer, doing an internet search using the words "Shady Rest" in quotes, followed by "Fredericksburg, Virginia," and finally the word "fire." Within two seconds he found exactly what he was looking for. He clicked the link and read a newspaper account of the fire.

He learned that the Shady Rest was not exactly a rehabilitation or convalescent center but was actually a sort of insane asylum. It only permitted non-violent offenders to reside there for community safety reasons, but something had gone very wrong. One of their guests, as they referred to them, rather than inmates, had an undocumented violent past. The man's name was Mason Tennyson.

Mason was apparently sent to Shady Rest under court order to be analyzed to determine where best to send him for his actual treatment. Mason was a pyromaniac who had been arrested for setting numerous fires around town, which resulted in thousands of dollars worth of damage.

The authorities were not aware of anyone being hurt in any of the fires, but of course they didn't know about all of his other fire-related activities. For example, they did not know about the hundreds of stray cats and dogs he had burned to death or the several homeless people he had kidnapped, taken into the woods, tied to trees, and set ablaze.

Apparently, one night while the residents of the Shady Rest slept, Mason went from room to room setting fires. The fires quickly raged out of control turning the Victorian era mansion into a furious inferno. Mason tried to escape through a side window but found its shutters locked closed, blocking his escape. The raging fire had blocked him from leaving the room as well. All tolled, seventy-five people perished in the fire including Mason Tennyson, whose charred body was found stuck fast to the window shutter where it burned as he struggled for fresh air while trying to escape the inferno.

Eddie's breath caught in his throat as he realized that the shutter out in the hall had to be the very shutter to which Mason Tennyson's body had been fused. He realized much more than the crazy man's flesh had been merged with the shutter, but his very essence, his evil soul had become one with the shutter as well. And now that wicked spirit had invaded the sanctuary of his home.

Eddie jumped up from his chair and raced across the room throwing open the office door. He could now hear the maniacal laughter louder and more evil than ever before. As he stared at the shutter hanging on the wall, the face once again began to appear in the background. It seemed to have three dimensions as if it were rising up from the surface of the shutter. It was charred black, and its burned flesh hung in smoldering chunks from its exposed soot-covered skull. The large white eyes seemed to bulge from their sockets, as all that still remained around them were the fleshless orbital bones.

Next, two   charred hands emerged from the background, their bones jutting from burned flesh which was barely existent. Within seconds the creature's entire torso extended out from the shutter, its artwork now engulfed in a mass of white-hot flames.

Maxine heard the commotion and came down the hall toward Eddie screaming with horror at the site unfolding before her. With one quick movement of its hand the specter of Mason sent a ball of fire down the hall striking Maxine square in the chest, spreading instantly all over her body, engulfing her in flames. Eddie watched in terror as Maxine's flesh began to drip like tallow from her still standing body, her once lovely eyes melting like marshmallows, running from her skull.

Before Eddie could react, the creature now laughing like the madman it once was, sent a ball of fire in his direction and after a few agonizing seconds of searing pain, only darkness remained.

Soon the entire house was ablaze, and before the fire company could arrive, it was completely engulfed and unable to be saved.

Several days later after the fire investigators had completed their work, two local vagrants were sifting through the remains hoping to find something valuable. One of them stumbled upon the shutter laying face down among the wreckage.

"Hey. What's this?" The one man asked.

The other replied, "It looks like a shutter, you know, for a window."

"What's it doing inside the house? Shouldn't it be on the outside?" He replied.

"Don't you know nothin'?" the second man replied. "It's like a decoration. Something people hang on their walls like a painting. Hell, it probably had something painted on it one time."

The first vagrant looked down at the shutter then flipped if over. "Holy Mary Mother of God!" The man screamed as he backed away from the shutter.

"Oh dear Lord," the other man cried as he, too, saw the image on the shutter.

The shutter was charred completely black. Three faces seemed to rise from the surface as if sculpted from a solid piece of wood. Two near the bottom of the shutter were of a man and a woman, both of whom seemed to be contorted in horror as if screaming in agony. Their faces were scorched and burned flesh seemed to hang in flaps from their charred skulls. Two skeletal hands held each of the images by their heads, leading upward to a third image. It was that of a wild-eyed burned and scarred man who appeared to be laughing hysterically, his eyes wide with insanity.

From Below

The beat up circa 1970s Chevy van eased its way to the curb in an abandoned area of the city so decayed and desolate not even the craziest of the city's walking wounded, nor the homeless street people or not even the most brain-fried of the crack-heads would go near it. It was, by far, one of the worst areas of the city. Locals often quipped, if one were to take the time to look up "urban blight" in the encyclopedia, he should not be at all surprised to find pictures of that district prominently displayed.

During the early part of the twentieth century, this four-block region along the river had been a booming garment district, with many multistoried clothing factories, employing thousands of people. There were also a few buildings set up for light manufacturing and assembly as well. Millions of dollars were made here for the owners of the businesses and the workers were always paid a fair wage, resulting in the building of hundreds of nearby row-homes and apartment buildings. Neighborhoods quickly began to spring up, and just as rapidly began filling with immigrants flocking to the city in search of employment.

However, things started to decline in the late 1950s and early 1960s as the labor unions became stronger and the wages became higher, while foreign competition flooded the market with dirt cheap products. Somehow a few of the businesses managed to hold on, at least for a while.

Then throughout the late 1970s and early 1980s, much of the work began to leave the country for places like China, Malaysia, Thailand, and Mexico while here the businesses were saddled with harsh fines and government imposed environmental regulations. Some businesses were accused of dumping harmful toxic chemicals and dyes into the river, which had the potential of polluting the neighborhood water system.

By the end of the decade in 1989, it was all over but the shouting, as all of the businesses had either moved their operations to foreign countries or had simply gone belly-up. The job market dried up, and the huge buildings were left abandoned. Soon the local neighborhoods were likewise left deserted, as former mill workers fled the area in search of new employment.

It was not long afterward that the urban decay began in earnest as the criminal elements of society moved in and vandals started breaking windows and looting whatever scraps they could from the abandoned buildings. Occasionally they started random fires, which quickly escalated into blazing infernos, turning both the local residences and factory buildings into burned out hulks; skeletal remains of what were once thriving and noble structures.

Then it wasn't long before the druggies and the crazies moved in; squatting and trying to survive among what little shelter the ruined buildings were able to provide. However, something drastically changed in the area during that time, near the end of the twentieth century. No one ever said for certain what had driven everyone away but it had to have been something so horrible; it was apparently terrifying enough to scare off even those most depraved characters, which were often considered on the bottom of the societal dung heap. And as a result, this mysterious unknown phenomenon had prevented any others from venturing into the area as well.

Even local gangs with the most violent of hardened criminals chose to avoid the menacing, disreputable buildings. It was as if the place was marked, or cursed somehow, and word of mouth obviously must have spread among the lowest of the low, because seldom was it anymore that even a solitary soul could ever be seen within the four-block area, especially after the sun went down. There had been talk and rumors among the homeless people in surrounding shelters; stories of unsolved disappearances, missing friends, presumed dead but whose bodies were never found.

It didn't take long for the stories to reach urban legend status, as people began to speak of "sightings" of creatures, possibly human, but perhaps not quite, who apparently controlled the area from their subterranean lairs. The tales said the creatures hunted and murdered their victims, cannibals devouring anyone they came upon. The lurid stories never quite made it out of the city into the suburbs, however, since the two cultures seldom, if ever had any opportunity to comingle. So, on occasion, groups of young people from the 'burbs would wander into the burned out ruins seeking adventure. Most of them were never were seen again.

The weather-beaten van idled at the curb, shaking slightly from the vibration of the ancient engine chugging persistently, giving the van the appearance of trembling in terror, which was apropos for a place with such an ominous reputation.

Inside the van, the driver, a young man named Cameron Johns, turned to look at his best friend Chase, who was seated on the passenger side.

"So here we are," Cameron said with a slight bit of unease in his voice.

Chase didn't seem to notice Cameron's discomfort, and turned to look into the back of the van where two girls sat awkwardly on a pair of oversized bean bag chairs. "Well, ladies, are you ready for this?"

"I'll tell you one thing," the girl named Crystal said from the dark back of the van, "I'm most certainly ready to get out of this potentially syphilitic, AIDS infested death trap you call a van."

"Hey!" Cameron retorted. "Careful how you talk about my . . . love machine."

"Right," the other girl, Jen, replied. "This piece of garbage may have been a shaggin' wagon back in its day, but it stopped being a love machine the day you bought it."

"Whoa!" Cameron said, "That's harsh! You know, ordinarily that would hurt my feelings—"

"—if it wasn't so true," Chase interrupted.

He and the two girls laughed hysterically while Cameron sat sulking, pretending to be insulted. The group often took turns exchanging barbs; it was simply a part of their special relationship. Then Chase asked, still chuckling, "Cameron, why don't you tell the girls about that burnt out old hippy dude who sold you this piece of shit."

"Chase!" Crystal scolded from the back seat. "Language! Please! You know I am trying to keep my aura clean and pure by avoiding such negative and crude language." Crystal was bit of a flaky sort of personality, who seemed to bounce from one new age religion to another. The other members of their group assumed that with a name like Crystal, and two former earth-children hippy parents, it was inevitable that she would follow such a path in constant search of enlightenment.

Most recently she had discovered some new form of cosmic mysticism, and after reading several books on the occult, decided she was reincarnated from an Egyptian princess, although having failed geography she most likely didn't even know where Egypt was. She also fancied herself as a sort of medium, even though she had absolutely no clairvoyant abilities whatsoever. She dressed in a strange hodgepodge of various fashions from Bohemian to Far Eastern and even Gothic, depending upon her mood. This strange choice of garb tended to produce unusual looks from just about everyone who saw her.

The four were part of a group of five close friends who had known each other since grade school and all shared one thing in common; they didn't fit in anywhere socially but within this special cadre of like minds.

"Whatever," Chase replied to Crystal's rebuke. "Come on, Cameron. Tell them about the old guy . . . that smelly hippy dude."

Cameron laughed in spite of himself, and said, "This dude was so time-warped. He was like sixty-some years old and the guy still wore tie-dye shirts and had this long white goatee and Fu-Manchu mustache. He was like totally bald, with just this weird ring of white frizzy hair around his head. He must have tried hard to hang onto his long hair forever 'cause he had like five hairs that were about a mile long, all wrapped together in a ratty looking ponytail." The group laughed while Cameron continued, enjoying their reactions. "He said he was the original owner of the van and told me if the van could talk, boy could it tell some wild tales."

Crystal squirmed uncomfortably in her beanbag chair, tucking her legs tighter up under herself, not certain she wanted any of her clothing or heaven forbid, her flesh to come in contact with the worn shag carpet surrounding her conspicuously. Her stomach turned when she thought of the amount of spent DNA most likely still lingering in the fibers.

"He told me he always wanted to give the van a Viking funeral when it finally died," Cameron explained, "You know, take it out in a field and burn it when he couldn't drive it anymore. But he said it just kept running."

"So why did he want to sell it?" Jen asked, not seeming to mind sitting so close to the carpet as Crystal had. Jen was a bit more tom-boyish than Crystal and always seemed to be on a level playing field when it came to dealing with the boys at school. So she was not really fazed by the van's disreputable history or the thought of what disgusting elements might be lurking in the deep pile of shag carpet.

"Get this," Cameron said with a smile, continuing with his tale. "The dude got into some trouble with the cops for growing weed in his back yard and now he has a bunch of legal bills to pay. So the van had to go 'cause he needed the cashola. I picked it up for a song."

Crystal interjected, "I wouldn't be surprised if that song you bought it for was a funeral dirge. This thing is a dump on wheels."

Cameron countered, "It might seem like a dump to you and might be a bit rough around the edges, but it got us here tonight, didn't it?"

"Yeah!" Chase retorted, "And speaking of which, are we doing this or not?"

The "this" to which Chase was referring, was a special Halloween adventure the boys had planned and suggested to the girls, who after some cajoling and daring had reluctantly agreed. The idea was they would go down in to the worst area of the city on a Saturday night of Halloween weekend, and go into one of the spookiest of the buildings, check it out, and stay there until after midnight.

The original plan was to stay all night, but they were all seniors in high school and the logistics of pulling off something like that with their parents was not even worth considering. It was tough enough to come up with the appropriate lies to be able to stay out past midnight. Cameron was the only one with a senior license, while the other three were still operating with their Cinderella tags, which meant no driving between eleven at night and five in the morning. In fact, the fifth member of the group, Stacey, couldn't get her parents to agree to let her come at all, so they were four instead of five.

And now here they were at nine pm in one of the seediest neighborhoods in the city, sitting at the curb in what at one time was a gorgeous metallic red Chevy Van with smoke colored moon windows and sunroof and chrome trim. But now it was just a faded shadow of its former self, held together with duct tape, primer, and badly applied body putty.

"So, which building are we going to explore?" Jen asked with some reservation.

Chase said, "Me and Cam were down here scoping them out last weekend and we decided that one over there would be a good one to try."

He pointed across the street to a particularly gruesome looking structure, whose name was still displayed proudly in the carved granite slab suspended over the gaping mouth-like front opening, reading Martinson Fashions.

"My grandfather told me that way back in the early 1930s this factory was a real money maker," Cameron explained. "He said old man Martinson died a multi-millionaire and none of his kids or grandkids had to work a day of their lives."

Cameron continued, "This place was such a big deal, it had its own subway stop in the basement, so workers from all over the city could work here. The subway service stopped coming to this neighborhood back in the 1980s when the line shut down, but the platform is probably still there, somewhere under the building."

"And now look at it," Crystal said sadly. "It is a rundown wreck of a building. That is so sad."

"It's not sad, Crystal," Chase explained. "It is just business. The strong survive and the weak . . . well the weak end up looking like that building over there."

Jen spoke up, "So are you guys sure you checked this place out good enough? I mean, I don't want us running into a bunch of dopers or perverts or God know what in there."

"Yeah," Chase said. "Me and Cam scoped it out a couple times during the day and it's totally empty and pretty safe as long as you stay on the main path and don't go off on your own and end up falling down an elevator shaft or some shit like that."

"Chase! Your language!" Crystal shouted again.

"For Christ's sake, Crystal." Jen hollered back. "Stop worrying so much about your frickin' aura."

"Jen! Language!" Crystal admonished, shaking her head while Jen just threw her hands up in the air, and the boys simply rolled their eyes, smiling understandably.

Cameron announced, "OK everybody, it's now or never. Let's take this show on the road." With that, he opened the driver's door while Chase simultaneously opened the passenger door and got out on the abandoned street. Chase opened the sliding side door so the girls could get out as well. Crystal seemed to be repulsed and terrified every time she had to make contact with any part of the van, as if the beanbag chair was a raft in the middle of the ocean, surrounded by sharks.

Within a few moments the quartet of friends found themselves standing in front of what was, at one time, two enormous glass doors leading to the wrecked lobby of Martinson Fashions. The doors were completely gone, not even the metal framework or hinges remained. The doorway was charred black from one of the many fires that had been set throughout the years in this part of the city.

As they were about to enter the building Jen asked, "Does anyone have anything with them we can use to defend ourselves, like a flashlight or a gun or something?"

"Where the hell would I get a gun?" Cameron asked. Crystal gave him a disapproving look but he ignored her. "I do have a flashlight, though." He raised his Maglight flashlight to show the group.

"Me too!" Chase said showing his Maglight, which was a slightly larger model then Cameron's. "Hey look, Cam, mine is bigger than yours," Chase said as they both laughed.

"Oh my God!" Jen said shaking her head, "Flashlight envy!" Then she and Crystal chuckled conspiratorially. Jen explained, "Look. I just want to make sure if some doper or pervert or ax murder is hiding somewhere in there, we have some way to get out in one piece."

"Oh yeah," Chase continued, "I also have a pocket knife in case we need it."

"Wow!" Crystal interjected sarcastically, "We have a regular arsenal on our hands don't we?"

"Look," Cameron said, "There is nothing to worry about. No one is in there and there hasn't been anyone in there for years. The place is completely empty. There's nothing to worry about. Plus we all have our cell phones and we can call 911 anytime if we need to."

"I don't think the cops will come down to this part of town," Chase said putting his mouth in gear before his brain, as was typical.

"Good one, Chase!" Cameron admonished, "You are really doing a lot to help the cause."

Nevertheless, within a few minutes the four high school seniors were walking cautiously along a rubble strewn path inside the blackened lobby toward the back of the building.

"Watch out to your left," Cameron warned. "That is the empty elevator shaft I mentioned. You don't want to fall down there."

When they reached the back of the building they saw a doorway with a broken wooden door hanging suspended by one hinge. Stenciled on the front of the door, faded and charred was the word "Stairs."

"These are probably the stairs that lead down to the basement," Cameron said. "How cool would that be to see the old subway platform? We could take some pictures with our cell phones as proof we were here."

"Yeah," Jen said sarcastically, "and we could email them to all of our friends." She knew as well as the other three, there were no other friends. These four misfits and their missing friend Stacey were a unique group unto themselves. They often joked about their being different than everyone else and their lack of popularity at school. It never bothered them very much, until they thought about what might happen after graduation, when they each went their separate ways to start their own lives. They all swore to keep in contact but knew their close bond of friendship would eventually end and their lives would go on.

Cameron took a cautious step onto the top landing, shining his Maglight down the steep descending stairs. At first he jumped slightly, startled when he thought he saw something ducking back into the darkness just beyond the reach of his beam.

"Cam? Are you alright? You flinched," Crystal said.

"Yeah," Cameron replied. "It was nothing. This place just gives me the creeps."

"Me too," Jen said.

"Me three," Crystal said.

Chase looked surprised at them and said, "Well, isn't that what it's supposed to do? It's Halloween weekend and we are in probably the spookiest building in the city. Duh! We are supposed to be getting the creeps!"

"Yeah. Well it is working," Cameron replied.

They started their slow descent down the long stairway with Cameron still in the lead, being extremely vigilant to assure he had not really seen anything, other than perhaps a rat or one of the other many possible small, harmless animals that tended to live in abandoned buildings.

When they got to the bottom of the stairway they noticed it took a sharp left turn before continuing down another long flight of stairs.

"Holy shit!" Chase exclaimed. "How far down does this go?"

"Chase!" Crystal admonished. "Do you kiss your mother with that filthy mouth?"

He looked at her slyly and said, "I most certainly do and I would be happy to do the same for you sometime, sweet cheeks, but with much more enthusiasm."

"In your dreams," Crystal replied. "In your dreams."

As the group reached the bottom of the stairway, it again took another sharp left and led to another long set of stairs leading downward.

"What the hell?" Crystal exclaimed. The three friends looked at her with astonishment as she corrected herself. "I mean heck. I meant what the heck."

"Jesus, Crystal!" Jen said. "If you meant to say hell then say hell. Your stupid aura will be just as tarnished if you meant one thing and say some stupid substitute instead."

Crystal replied, "I know . . . it's just—"

"Wait a minute!" Chase interrupted. "What was that noise?"

"What noise?" Cameron asked. "I didn't hear anything."

Jen replied angrily, "Stop it, Chase! Stop being a douche bag. It's spooky enough down here without you trying to scare us. OK?"

"Honest, Jen," Chase explained. "I'm not being a dick or anything. I really thought I heard something. But now maybe I'm not so sure."

"Look," Cameron said, "we are two floors underground in an empty building. There are bound to be rats or mice or things like that running around down here. And you know how everything echoes in a stairway like this. Just relax, everything is OK."

Soon they reached the bottom of the third flight of stairs and saw another opening that led to almost total blackness, except for a slight bit of ambient lighting apparently coming from moonlight filtering in from some of the many holes in the high ceiling of the structure. The eerie light gave the area a dark gray, ominous appearance as surrounding features were hidden in black shadows. As they stepped out through the doorway, Cameron noticed the door to this passageway was still intact and appeared functional as it hung open. It was an old thick heavy metal thing, perhaps iron, that looked like it may have been installed for security purposes. They assumed it hadn't done much good as it now hung completely open.

Cameron continued to take the lead, followed by Jen, then Crystal, while Chase stayed in back. The boys had agreed to this arrangement before picking up the girls, figuring if they kept the girls in sight, between them, there was less chance of them accidentally getting hurt.

As they walked several feet, they all noticed a number of things. First they heard their footfalls echoing on the concrete floor as if indicating they had entered a very large room or chamber. They also noticed the vile stench of decomposition, as if something had died as was rotting nearby.

"Oh my God! What stinks? Where the hell are we?" Jen asked, feeling as if she would vomit.

"I think we are in the basement on the subway platform," Cameron said. The group continued to walk steadily forward as Cameron led the way with his flashlight scanning the area.

Chase likewise was surveying the concrete platform, which appeared vast and empty. Suddenly his light reflected off of something just beyond the expanse of concrete to his right. No one else was looking in that direction. He raised his beam slightly to try to get a better look. To his surprise he saw a pile of tattered remnants of old filthy clothing.

Then he was horrified to discover directly next to the pile of rags a mountain of what looked like bones—human bones. Rib cages, skulls, and the like were all piled chaotically, perhaps ten feet high. Rats crawled among the bones and Chase noticed one of the creatures in particular, poking his wiggling snout from the empty eye socket of one of the broken skulls. Chase wanted to cry out but his voice caught in his throat as his stomach retched in disgust.

Before he could regain his composure and warn the others of what he had just seen, he felt a searing pain for just a moment as a sharp hooked and barbed arrowhead entered through the back of his neck and passed right through him creating a massive tear in the front of his throat, severing his carotid artery on exit. The last thing he saw before his eyes went black under the shroud of death was his three friends silhouetted in Cameron's flashlight walking slowly away, oblivious to his fate.

Someone had fastened a rope crudely to the back end of the arrow. Within a second, an unseen force from somewhere back in the darkness yanked quickly on the line, pulling Chase's corpse backward into the blackness. The three friends heard Chase's flashlight fall with a clang to the concrete floor and they quickly turned around as one to see what had happened. They saw nothing but blackness behind them and Chase's flashlight slowly rolling about in a circular motion, its beam randomly scouring the darkness.

"Chase!" Crystal screamed, her voice immediately filling with terror and the certain realization something very bad had happened to their friend. Cameron pointed the light back into the darkness as he hurried past the girls toward the fallen flashlight. The flashlight stopped its circular motion and lay perfectly still, shining its beam back toward the stairway door they had passed through after coming down from the main level.

As he got closer to the flashlight he stopped in his tracks, stricken with terror at the vision which lay before him. At the spot where Chase had previously stood Cameron saw a huge sickening crimson patch of blood, with drag marks smearing backward away from him, indicating the bloody path by which Chase's body had apparently been dragged.

Cameron turned to the girls shining his flashlight on them and screamed, "Get the hell out of here. Get upstairs and call for help! Now!"

Without a moment's hesitation, Jen sprinted past Crystal heading for the open doorway illuminated by Chase's flashlight beam. Her right hand already had her cell phone out as she quickly dialed 911. However, nothing happened. She stopped suddenly at the door to the stairs and looked down at her phone display screen only to see in frustration that she had no service. "No!" she screamed to herself. "We're three floors underground. I have to get upstairs." As she turned to re-enter the stairway she looked back toward her two friends just as she heard Crystal scream.

The sight that followed was something worse than any nightmare she had ever experienced. In the light from Cameron's quaking flashlight, still pointing at Crystal, six or ten thin naked muscular arms seemed to come from the darkness behind her, encircling her, grabbing her. Two of the hands, filthy with grime were grabbing her head, pulling it backward, their long-nailed fingers digging into her eye sockets. Jen watched helplessly as Crystal's eyeballs popped like squashed grapes, while at the same time another set of hands, ripped her shirt from her body and gouged long bloody furrows across her exposed breasts and abdomen. As the girl was pulled back into the darkness, Jen saw another arm with long claw-like fingers reach around the girl's neck and literally rip her throat out, as Crystal's scream faded into a ghastly liquid-like death rattle.

"Cameron! Come on!" Jen shouted as the boy stood apparently in shock, perhaps petrified by the horrible spectacle he had just witnessed. Then Jen saw the truth as a small red patch appeared at the front of his shirt, rapidly growing in size as his life blood drained from him. Cameron looked down at the spot as if dumfounded. Then he slowly turned to Jen and he mouthed the word "go" before collapsing face forward to the concrete.

Jen quickly turned and started running up the stairs, taking two at a time, all the while occasionally glancing down at her phone with the hopes of finding available service, but so far she had none. Behind her she could hear wild chattering sounds, not of any language she had ever heard but nonetheless it sounded like some type of verbal communication. She also heard what sounded like hundreds of footfalls coming up the stairs behind her. She stumbled several times during her ascent but always managed to keep going out of sheer terror. She knew if she stopped her fate would be in the murderous hands of the unknown creatures pursuing her.

It seemed like her lungs would burst from her sprint up the three flights of stairs, but at last she saw some light from the street shining through the doorway up ahead, indicating she had almost made it to the first floor. She ventured a glance at her cell phone and saw to her pleasure she once again had full service. She quickly pressed 911 and then the call button as she rounded the corner at the top of the stairway, heading for the lobby.

When she entered the open area, Jen stopped in her tracks, unable to believe the sight before her. The lobby was full of horribly deformed not quite human looking creatures all caked with filth, and dried blood. Some were dressed in the most minimal of scraps of clothing while others were completely naked.

Several of the pathetic creatures seemed to possess shortened almost flipper-like arms and legs, while others were missing limbs completely; and still others appeared to have more limbs than normal. They all were hunched and twisted with various horrific facial deformities, and they spoke in some strange tongue, which they seemed to understand, though she did not. And the stench coming from the things was unlike anything Jen had ever smelled before. It was as if the room was suddenly filled with dead and rotting animals.

She heard a voice come from her cell phone saying "911 operator. What is the nature of your emergency?" Before she could lift the cell phone to answer, sharp clawed hands grabbed her from behind, dragging her backward into the stairwell as the strange chattering sounds of the hideous creatures grew louder and louder. She suddenly felt excruciating pain as the flesh was stripped from her body. She had an image of a fish being flayed as the pain grew to an unbearable agony. Then finally blessed death came to take her, and Jen could not hear another sound.

***

About twenty minutes later a police cruiser pulled up alongside the building, across the street from the abandoned van in response to the 911 call. Someone had triangulated the location of the still active cell phone. Two officers exited the van and looked up and down the street trying to determine if anyone was around. Their identification tags read Rossi and Flannery; two old school career beat cops. They walked over to the van, which was unlocked, and saw it was empty. Then they heard what sounded like faint speaking coming from inside one of the buildings.

They entered the building with their flashlights on, and could see the glowing screen in the distance by the rear of the building. They approached the phone and heard the 911 operator, keeping the line open and still trying to find someone to answer.

Rossi bent down, picked up the phone and said, "Hello."

The voice on the other end of the phone said, "Hello. This is the 911 operator. Is everything all right?"

Rossi attempted to speak again into the phone to identify himself, but his partner, Flannery could only hear a faint hissing sound coming from the man's mouth. He saw a look of utter disbelief and pain on Rossi's face, as the man stood still, holding the phone with is mouth agape. Then a small trickle of blood spilled down his chin from the corner of his mouth. When Flannery looked down at his partner's chest, he saw the sharp point of some sort of arrow tip jutting out, covered with blood, bits of flesh and gore. A second later his partner disappeared as if pulled off of his feet by some incredible force and propelled through the air, back into the darkness.

Flannery lifted his left hand to press his shoulder radio as his right hand dropped to his side, pulling his gun from its holster. Before his hand could reach the button of this radio, his arm was severed above the elbow by some sort of flying disk. As his blood pumped from his body, Flannery looked straight ahead and could see what looked like hundreds of glowing red eyes emerging from the darkness. It was the last thing he would ever see.

In the next several days, police conducted an investigation to try to determine what had happened to the missing teens as well as the two police officers. They did a thorough search of the area and brought in a forensic team, who identified the bloodstains found in the lobby as being the same blood type as those of Jen as well as officers Rossi and Flannery. They never found any bodies or evidence of what had happened to the other missing teens.

During the search several officers had ventured down the long three-story stairway to the basement but found the huge iron door leading to the subway platform closed, apparently barred from the other side, and incapable of being opened. They agreed that no one could have gotten through the door. They accepted the futility of trying to force the door open and abandoned their search, heading for the surface.

They were correct, of course. The door could not be opened, at least not from the stairway side. You see, the door could only be opened from the platform side and was only ever opened by the mutated former humans from below. And they only opened the door at night—at their feeding time.

Saw-Kill Road

The forlorn two-lane blacktop road snaked like a writhing serpent over its short half-mile length from end to end, connecting the busy Abington Lane with the mountainous Prescott Road. Its narrow winding progression curved past the abandoned, once prosperous saw mill from which the road attained its name, "Sawmill Road." However, its unofficial moniker was much more menacing—known to locals, especially the children as "Saw-Kill Road."

At the start of the twentieth century, the sawmill had been a bustling enterprise, employing a number of local men; once a large two-story clapboard building, the wood sealed to allow its weather-resistance to fight off the elements.

Where the mill was level with the roadway two large barn-style doors opened to a dirt drive. As the land sloped downward, a stone foundation reached five feet high to support the building and provided a doorway access to a basement storage area, as well as windows for light. The ceiling of the basement area was comprised of thick wooden beams, serving also as the floor for the sawmill itself.

Above the beautiful oak front door with its solid brass door knocker and crystal door knob was a transom which held a custom made stain glass window bearing the name "Hanson's Mill" in honor of the former owner of the mill, Jonas Jackson Hanson, known as "J.J." to what few friends he had, and "the cheap limy bastard" to most of his employees.

Now, the mill stood in decay; its once beautiful wooden siding putrefying from years of exposure to the elements, fading to whitish gray, rotten and infested with insects. Rusted hinges hung loosely from disintegrating clapboards, some of them hanging by a single remaining corroded screw; a sad reminder of a time long ago when the mill's shutters hung proudly. Now, not only were all of the shutters long gone, but most of the remaining glass panes had been either removed or shattered, leaving sharp jagged fragments in the frames, resembling hideous shark teeth. A few may have been stolen by thieves hoping to get something for the custom blown panes, but most were simply broken by local vandals, for whatever enjoyment they might gain from such thoughtless actions. Behind the broken windows awaited nothing but the blackness of the abandoned structure and whatever else might lurk inside in the darkness.

The once magnificent front door had likewise long since been stolen, allowing an opening for a variety of woodland creatures to wander into the mill to take up residence. Perhaps the missing door was currently being used as someone's front door in a mansion in another state or another country, or maybe it had simply been burned for firewood. Its fate remained a mystery as did much about the mill. Where the stained glass transom once proudly displayed the mill owner's name, nothing remained but an empty pitted wooden frame covered in spider webs, teaming with insects, many of which would no doubt eventually end up cocooned in gossamer awaiting digestion by the families of spiders.

At one time, a large double-sided fireplace was located in the middle of the mill providing heat for the workers in the winter. It led to an enormous chimney stretching high above the center of the roofline, making for breathtaking spectacle as it spewed its smoke into the icy sky during the coldest, most frigid months. Now the chimney was all but gone above the roofline, its mortar disintegrated by years of exposure to the elements, its bricks having fallen to the ground below; many plummeting through the roof itself, making large gaping holes in the rotting cedar shake shingles.

Through the center of the chimney, large branches grew skyward from an oak tree that had taken root a few years after the mill had been shut down. Branches likewise protruded through the broken windows looking as if the tree and its massive limbs might be the only thing keeping the mill standing; which could very well have been true.

The locals called it "Saw-Kill" because of the mill's tragic history, or perhaps more accurately, the tragic history of the mill's owner, J. J. Hanson. The tale of Jonas J. Hanson had been a sad one when told with historic accuracy. However, through the years the tale had grown and evolved, each time being told with the addition of more fantastic and even impossible elements, until it had become the stuff of legend. It was no longer simply a tragic tale but one of terror and mystery.

Jonas had been the only child of a British father and a German mother who had immigrated to the United States toward the end of the nineteenth century. Shortly after his arrival, Jonas's father, William, built the mill and began growing his business. Jonas was born in 1880, and by the turn of the century the mill had become a very prosperous business. Jonas took over ownership and operation of the mill in 1905, at the age of twenty-five when his father died suddenly. A heart attack had truly been the cause of his father's untimely death, but through the years a number of rumors and stories came into being suggesting that perhaps young Jonas had actually murdered his father to get control of the mill. It didn't seem to matter that the stories were complete fabrications; many people believed them to be true.

The bottom line was, the workers didn't take well to Jonas running the operation, as they looked at him as having been privileged and being given everything as a result of the hard work of his father's success. They all respected and had great admiration for William, as he was not only hardworking and intelligent but was generous to a fault. He always put the welfare of his workers before profit.

Such was not the case for Jonas. He knew how his employees felt about him, but he didn't care. So instead of trying to win the workers over and gain their respect, Jonas took a firm, autocratic approach, driving his workers with an iron fist, firing anyone who gave him even the slightest provocation. The economy was not prosperous in the poor rural Pennsylvania community, as was often the case in such areas, so the employees had little choice but to put up with Jonas's tyranny or starve. They may have started out disliking Jonas, but soon they despised him.

Jonas never married or had any children. He took over the family homestead, a large farmhouse on the same parcel of land, but located several hundred yards in the woods behind the mill. His mother, Greta, lived in the house with him until she died of cancer, then known as "the waste of life," around 1925. Jonas soon found himself alone, in the big house and did not consider the isolation comforting.

Locals rumored that his mental decline started after his mother's death. Many said the spirits of the dead parents haunted the homestead, tormenting Jonas relentlessly because of his poor treatment of the workforce. That particular rumor was probably started by a group of irate workers who hated Jonas and simply wished deep inside, such an impossible phenomenon might actually have occurred.

Others, who dared to be so vulgar, hinted about an unnatural intimate relationship between Jonas and his mother after his father's death, which caused him to go mad with grief following her subsequent passing. Whatever the reason, after a number of years alone in the "big house," as it was known, Jonas started to act irrationally and could often be seen carrying on conversations with people who were not present; some said he was speaking with his dead mother and father. This probably helped to fuel the ghost rumors as well.

Eventually, for whatever reason, Jonas lost his mind completely. Unfortunately, no one realized the extent of his insanity until it was much too late. Until then, most of his employees simply thought of him as being a bit "off," and chose to ignore his steady mental decline in order to remain gainfully employed at the mill.

Then one day it happened. After the long workday had ended and most of the workers had gone home, Jonas was hunched over his desk in his office, mumbling to himself as usual, working on the business's books. A group of four obviously angry workers approached him demanding to speak to him about the working conditions. When he refused to talk with the men, they told Jonas they were in the process of forming a labor union and he would either have to give in to their demands or they would be forced to call a strike and would shut the mill down.

Even though most of what they said was simply bluster, they had started talking among themselves about the possibility of forming a union. Though they were actually years away from making it a reality, Hanson was unaware of this. And in his deteriorated mental state he couldn't distinguish between what portion of their threat was real and what might be contrived.

He snapped. While the four men were spelling out their demands he reached into the top drawer of his desk, retrieved a Smith and Wesson .38 special revolver and proceeded to shoot each of them without a second of forethought. One of the men died instantly when the bullet entered just above his right eye, blowing out the back of his skull and spattering his blood and bits of skull and brain all over the back wall of the office.

One of the men took one through the neck and lay on the floor gasping for several long minutes as his severed carotid artery pumped his lifeblood onto the floor where it pooled about him, soaking into the planking. The other two workers were not so lucky. Though one was shot once and the other twice their wounds were crippling but not fatal. In reality, they would have been much better off had they died instantly like their partners. The two men screamed in agony and tried to crawl toward the door desperately struggling to get away from the homicidal mad man.

Unfortunately, they didn't see him grab a souvenir baseball bat, which was presented to him by a customer and company that purchased his lumber to make their sports equipment. He shattered both of their legs so they couldn't escape, then broke their arms and dislocated their shoulders so they could not fight back. Whether he originally planned to kill them with the bat or whether he changed his mind during the process no one would ever know for certain. But the result was he only knocked them both unconscious.

When the men finally regained consciousness they found themselves inside the sawmill, strapped to the huge saw table, legs spread as the belts above the table spun on their pulleys, powering the enormous saw blade, causing it to whirr above the table directly in front of them. Then the blade began its journey down toward them preparing to split them from crotches to their skulls, and within a few moments the screaming and thrashing was over, as each half of the workers separated and collapsed to the table top, which became slick with their blood, entrails, and stomach contents.

Apparently, Jonas had saved one bullet for himself, and after his gruesome work was completed he went back to his office, sat behind his desk, put the barrel of the gun into his mouth and pulled the trigger The police investigating the crime scene were sickened by the manner in which he fell face-forward on top of his desk, his sodden brains oozing out onto a photo of his parents, which had fallen over and lay beneath his ruined skull.

***

Paul Simmons was a twenty-first century transplant to the area, but knew about the history of the mill, having heard local children discussing it while they played in the streets of his nearby suburban neighborhood. He and his wife, Laura, had only recently built their split-level home, having completed it several months earlier. Theirs was one of the last lots remaining in an already established development. Paul and Laura were both professionals, referred to as D.I.N.K.s by their coworkers; double income —no kids. They both wanted to have children someday, but so far they had not attempted to conceive.

During the workweek, they both attended a nearby gym and fitness center, but on the weekends, weather permitting, they enjoyed walking along the country roads near their new neighborhood. They would leave the development and head east on Abington Lane until they reached Sawmill. Then they would walk the half-mile length of the road, past the sawmill; unconsciously keeping their distance from the ruins. Next they would turn right on Prescott Road and follow it until it intersected with the very steep Dairy Road, which eventually met back up with Abington Lane on the other side of their development, completing about a two mile circle.

Often, when he would walk by the mill, Paul would deliberately stare at the structure, thinking about the stories surrounding the mill's history. He suspected that what he had heard might be close to what really happened although it was likely that the truth had been blown way out of proportion throughout the years. He often felt a strange, uneasy sensation in his stomach when passing the mill. Sometimes he even imagined that there might be some unearthly force calling to him; urging him to come inside the mill and investigate.

Most of the locals believed or wanted to believe the place was haunted. Many stories suggested that the ghost of J. J. Hanson wandered about the inside the mill, his spirit still insane and looking for another victim to saw in two. Paul, of course, refused to allow himself to even consider believing in such local folklore, thinking it ridiculous. Even the nickname "Saw-Kill" sounded juvenile and corny to him. In fact, he was fairly sure once, several years ago, when he and Laura had lived in California, he had seen a sign in a seasonal Halloween store reading "Saw-Kill Road."

As he recalled it was one of those cheap foam or cardboard road signs, probably mass-produced in China or some other low-cost country, for a US company eager for cheap labor. The sign had been designed with a green background and reflective white lettering, just like a typical road sign would be. It read "Saw Mill Road," however the "Mill" portion of the sign was obscured by the scribbled word "KILL" done in a way to appear to be written with dripping blood. Paul was fairly certain neither the workers in China, the businessmen in the United States, or even the designers who created the idea for the sign had any prior knowledge of this particular Sawmill Road in Pennsylvania, or any knowledge of its ominous history.

In fact, there were probably hundreds of Sawmill Roads around the country. Then he suddenly thought for a moment about a line he remembered from the promotion of the horror movie, "Nightmare on Elm Street," which read, "There's an Elm Street in every town." Paul figured there must also be a Sawmill Road in almost every rural community as well. Hence, the popularity of the novelty sign, he supposed.

As Paul became more familiar with the area he began to feel less apprehensive about the dilapidated building and eventually had no trouble walking past it. In fact, the previous day he had taken the walk alone as Laura was not feeling well. He deliberately slowed down as he got to the mill, bold enough to leave the road and walk up to the structure and stand within a few feet of its battered and rotted front stairs.

Now, a day later, he sat at the kitchen table having just finished his Sunday evening dinner and asked Laura if she was up for a walk; he suspected she might not yet be ready for one, as she hadn't seemed to eat very much at dinner.

"No." She replied, "I'm still not feeling so well in my stomach. It must just be a bug or something. If I don't feel much better by tomorrow morning, I suspect I'll have to stay home from work and go to the doctor."

Paul thought how odd it was to hear Laura consider staying home since she rarely missed work no matter how sick she might be. "If you feel that bad, do you think we ought to take you to the emergency room?"

"No thanks," she said with a sarcastic laugh. "I would rather lie around here all night than spend five or six hours in a room full of sick and injured weekend warriors. You know how poor people always flock to the hospital for their medical needs. Do you remember the last time we were there? It seemed like most of the families knew each other; like it is a party they all go to every weekend or something."

"Yeah. I remember," Paul said, thinking about how about two months ago he had cut his finger doing yard work and Laura had to drive him into the hospital for stitches. It was a four-hour snore-fest before the physician's assistant even had an opportunity to look at his injury. "You're probably right."

"I think I'll just go in and lie down on the couch for a while and watch TV," Laura said.

"Would you mind if I took our Sawmill walk alone?" he asked. Laura looked out the window and noticed the sun was beginning to set. "Are you sure you want to do that?" she suggested, not wanting to express her apprehension about the waning light too strongly, feeling somewhat foolish at the thought of doing so.

Sure," he said. "In fact, I might even run part of the way to make sure I get back before dark. Don't worry, I'll be fine."

"I suppose, if you say so," Laura replied with discomfort. "Take your cell phone along with you in case you trip and fall or get hit by a car or something."

"I will," he said with confidence as he held up his phone to show her he would be just a phone call away. He walked her to the couch and made sure she was comfortable before kissing her goodbye.

Paul walked out the front door of their home and strode at a brisk pace through the development for about a half-mile until the cement sidewalks ended abruptly at Abington Lane. Checking for oncoming traffic, he crossed Abington to the right side of the road walking steadily until he came to the intersection with Sawmill.

"Saw-Kill" a quiet, raspy voice echoed in his head and he felt himself mouthing the words silently along with the thought.

As he turned right onto Sawmill Road, he felt a strange sensation, as if he not only had just stepped onto another road but was actually entering another world. He looked out along the curves of Sawmill, which seemed to take on a dreamlike, surrealistic appearance. Paul knew that just around the next turn in the road ahead the ominous saw mill awaited like a hideous specter lurking in the shadows as if in anticipation of his arrival.

For a moment, he thought perhaps he should simply turn around, head home. He could always tell Laura he was more tired than he had realized or he could say he got a cramp in his leg or some other type of lame excuse. But he knew if he did she might deduce the real reason why he didn't want to walk by the mill. Although Paul was certain Laura would understand completely, never call him on it, and most certainly not think less of him, he didn't like the idea of her knowing he had backed out. If he went home early she would always know he was unable to bring himself to walk by the mill alone as the sun began to set.

Paul decided instead, he would walk at a deliberate pace up Sawmill Road with his head focused on the highway in front of him and do everything he could to not change the direction of his vision until he was well past the mill. He actually considered jogging past the mill to get it over with more quickly, but felt somehow that doing so wouldn't be much different than if he had turned around and gone home. So instead, he walked with his eyes focused on the blacktop, purposefully moving up Sawmill Road. "Saw-Kill" he again heard a strange unfamiliar voice whisper in his mind. He tried desperately to ignore the strange voice, blaming it on an overactive imagination.

As he approached the area where the mill stood he heard the voice in his head grow stronger, taking on a tone that sounded eerily insane. "Saw-Kill" the voice said repeatedly; first slowly, growing louder and more frantic with each utterance; "Saw-Kill, Saw-Kill, Saw-Kill" over and over. Paul stopped in the middle of the road and slowly raised his head, turning it cautiously to the right where the decaying saw mill stood. Instantly, the voice that had been assaulting him inside his mind stopped and was replaced by blessed silence. As he looked at the opening where the front door of the mill once stood he saw a cavern of darkness resembling the gaping maw of some hideous demonic creature.

But regardless of the doorway's appearance, Paul realized the apprehension he had previously felt was now completely gone. In fact, he felt foolish for having the strange feelings in the first place. It was as if he suddenly realized the mill was an abandoned building, a run-down wreck, nothing more. He felt an incredible exhilaration flow through him as he stood in the diminishing sunlight of dusk in front of the community's most feared legend. He felt nothing but pity for the unfortunate, superstitious locals who allowed themselves to fall prey to such wild imaginings.

Before he realized he was doing so, Paul stepped off the roadway, through the tall weeds and wild grass, walking directly toward the front of the building. He stood for a moment looking up at the precarious structure as if defying it to collapse, which of course it did not.

He walked slowly around to the left side of the building and saw the dirt driveway leading up to the large entrance where once two barn doors stood. He walked up the pathway to the opening and was surprised to see that the floor of the mill still appeared to be fairly intact and structurally sound. He could see how the builders had obviously constructed the floor supports with thick wooden beams. He also noted there was still a fair amount of light in the mill streaming through the broken western-facing window panes as well as bright setting sun flooding in from the gaping holes in the building's roof.

Paul stepped cautiously out onto the floor, testing each step to assure himself that the structure was as sturdy as it appeared to be. Before he realized it, he had taken several steps inside the mill and was turning to look down the length of the building. To his surprise, twenty or thirty feet ahead, he saw a large worktable, above which hung a giant rusted and pitted circular saw blade from the legendary and notorious saw he had heard so much about. It was the same blade which local legends touted as the "saw of death." Looking up toward the ceiling, he could see where once the huge canvas drive belts, which had been used to power the blade, once hung. Now all that remained were just dry-rotted torn strips hanging limply like giant pieces of shredded noodles, useless for powering any machinery ever again—or so Paul thought.

He walked forward toward the work table and as he looked down he noticed a dark brown stain soaked into the wooden slab. Looking upward more closely at the rusted circular blade, he saw a similar dark stain. Blood, Paul thought. A bloodstain from the last night the saw was ever used. Once again, the uncontrollable shiver returned and Paul felt a pang of apprehension at the resurgence of his earlier fears.

As Paul stared in amazement at the useless rusted blade, he noticed it begin to change. Before his eyes, the rust began to flake off in thousands of tiny bits of falling debris and orange dust, revealing a shiny metal blade below the surface. The dark area encircling the teeth of the blade was now bright red and drips of fresh blood began to fall from the blade's teeth to the bench below where it puddled, reflecting the last remaining glimmer of the setting sun. Paul could smell a coppery scent in the air and instinctively knew it was coming from the blood. Above him, the rotted sagging drive belts regained the luster of a new product and began to climb upward, all the while knitting themselves miraculously back together; repairing themselves right before his unbelieving eyes, and looking as if they were new.

Paul tried to turn and run from the nightmare unfolding before him but was unable to move. Suddenly he felt someone grab him from behind. He turned to try to see who held him and saw a portion of something he would have never believed possible. A translucent being stood behind him holding him securely, preventing him from escape. He was certain it was a thing of no substance, yet he could feel the impossible pressure of its icy fingers holding him in its death grip as an incredible coldness permeated his body. He couldn't quite make out the thing's appearance but sensed it must have looked hideous. He felt his heart pounding violently in his chest harder than he had ever felt before.

Then he heard a familiar voice in his mind. It was the same voice he had heard earlier saying, "Saw-Kill, Saw-Kill." He looked in the direction of the sound and saw someone slowly walking from the darkness toward him. It appeared to be a man dressed in early twentieth century clothing, a business suit that appeared to be stained with blood. As Paul looked closer he could see that the right side of the man's skull was missing and his face was splattered with chunks of skin and blood. Then Paul realized it was not really a man but some horrible specter made manifest before him. He realized it was that he was seeing was the ghost of J. J Hanson.

Behind the hideous ghost, another such creature of the damned came lumbering out of the blackness. The thing appeared to have once been a man, but now was something unimaginably hideous. This wretched creature stood naked with no visible genitalia. From the place where its crotch should have been, a long continuously twisting line of awkwardly sewn stitching worked its way up along the stomach area, past the chest, then the neck and finally passing through the center of its face and skull. Paul understood immediately that what he was seeing was what he had heard described in the local stories. It was one of the unfortunate workers Jonas had cut in two on the very table before him using the very circular blade that now glimmered overhead.

On the right side of its face the blade must have cut into the man's eye since the raggedly stitched path went up and through the empty black eye socket. Paul noticed the air in the mill had become thick with the stench of decay; a stink that turned his stomach and revolted him beyond description.

He then made the assumption that the creature holding him from behind must be the second of Jonas's victims. He still couldn't comprehend how these spirits had the ability to restrain him so. Then he suddenly understood. In reality, he was not actually being physically manhandled by the creatures but his subconscious mind believed it was happening and that was apparently sufficient to curtail his movements and make him feel as if the demon was actually touching him. One might say it was all in his head, yet he could not move any more than if the specter had been made of flesh and bone.

An involuntary scream built in Paul's throat but was cut off as he found himself unable to utter a sound. The shambling creature that stood next to the ghost of Jonas J. Hanson shambled jerkily forward and grabbed Paul's legs, somehow impossibly lifting them upward and placing them on the saw table. Unable to move or resist, Paul was helpless to do anything to free himself.

Within a few moments the saw blade rotate slowly at first; then it began to spin madly until it became a whirling blur spraying droplets of blood down upon him. Soon the blade moved ever so slowly downward, heading directly toward the center of Paul's chest. In his mind he heard a chorus of ghostly shrieks screaming, "Saw-Kill, Saw-Kill," repeatedly, just before everything went black.

***

Laura stood silently at the gravesite of her dead husband, dressed in widow's black, surrounded by friends and a few relatives. One by one, the mourners approached her to offer their condolences until soon all were gone and she found herself standing alone. That was, except for one lone man who lingered next to the grave. She recognized him immediately as the local medical examiner. He had told Laura he would tell her of his final determination of cause of death as soon as he had an answer. He was waiting to tell her of his findings.

The examiner approached Laura and said, "Once again, Mrs. Simmons, I am so very sorry for your loss."

"Thank you, Doctor Anderson. I appreciate it very much," she replied. Then wanting to get the unpleasantness over with quickly she asked, "I was wondering . . . did you finalize your report . . . you know . . . on Paul's cause of death? Was it . . . was it a heart attack?"

"Yes, my dear. That was the cause; a massive cardiac infarction. Unusual in one so young—but not unheard of. No one could have anticipated it. Again please accept my deepest sympathy," the doctor replied.

Laura's face took on the appearance of sad resignation that often accompanies the feeling of closure in such uncontrollable situations. "Thank you for all you have done, Doctor." Laura replied as the doctor nodded, turned, and left without further comment.

Walking slowly back to his car, the doctor saw his assistant waiting to drive him back to the office.

"Did you tell her?" the assistant inquired.

"I told her what she needed to hear," the doctor replied, "Her husband had a heart attack and that is why he died. End of story."

"But what about . . .?" the young assistant asked curiously stopping short of completing his question.

The doctor stared at him sternly and insisted, "I told her nothing. And as far as you and I are concerned, there is nothing else to tell; nothing to tell her and nothing to ever tell anyone else. And since you and I are the only two people who know the entire truth and we will never speak of it again the secret should remain a secret. Also, I had better never hear anyone else in this township repeating any such story back to me, or I will most certainly know exactly where it came from. Do I make myself perfectly clear?"

"Clear as clear can be," the assistant replied appropriately chastised. "I swear, I won't say a word about it to anyone."

With that, the doctor and his assistant got into their car and drove away in silence. The doctor went over in his mind the incredibly impossible results of his examination. It was beyond his understanding, beyond his comprehension how such a thing could possibly have occurred.

When he had autopsied Paul Simmons, he never expected to discover what he saw upon cracking open the man's chest cavity. No one ever would have anticipated finding the dead man's heart impossibly split cleanly in two.

Be Careful What You Wish For

*Be careful what you wish for because you
just might get it.*

—Unknown

*The only suitable gift for the man who has everything is
your deepest sympathy.*

—Imogene Fey

Protect me from what I want.

—Jenny Holzer

It had been yet another in a seemingly endless series of
monotonous days; a day just like every other boring day of
late and Stephen had become frustrated beyond his ability
to reason. He had had enough of walking about aimlessly
with no destination, no plan. Was this truly to be how he
would spend the rest of his natural life? He felt as if he
might lose his mind and scream with insanity just thinking
about how miserable his life had become. How it consisted
of the same old tiring routines day after day, week after
week for low these many years.

This was all the more frustrating because Stephen
knew he had enough money to be in complete control of
every aspect of his life—much more so than most people.
Nonetheless he continued to trudge along with the same
mundane daily routine without deviation. And although he
hated his life he did nothing to try to change it because he
knew it was of his own making and emotionally he no
longer had the ability to change anything. An outside
observer might say he had everything, but Stephen knew
in reality he had nothing, at least nothing that really
mattered to him any longer.

Stephen had fallen into an exceptionally deep pit of
depression having no idea how he might possibly go about

digging himself out and really no longer caring if he ever did. He had been depressed before, several times over the years but this time it seemed much worse than ever. The creeping bouts of malaise had slowly begun several years earlier shortly after it had all happened; after his pitifully bad luck had done an abrupt about face; that is to say, at least from an economic standpoint.

Now Stephen had the kind of financial good fortune most people only dreamed of. He had never even imagined having such vast amounts of money. However he knew if he could be granted just one wish, that is to say one more wish, it would be for everything to return to the way it had once been and all of what he now possessed would simply go away. But Stephen knew there would be no more wishes for him; those days were long gone. If he were going to find a way out of this miserable pit of despair he would have to do so of his own volition.

What Stephen did understand however was he had to come up with some means by which to put some sort of distraction or excitement into his life; something new; something to stimulate him; even if that something was something out of his control and potentially dangerous. He needed to find some activity that might possibly represent some sort of alteration to his normal mind-numbing practices; any sort of change whatsoever.

Stephen no longer worried about death or injury; his luck was much too good to allow something as trivial as physical injury to occur. He had tried all of the most hazardous of activities he could think of, from mountain climbing to sky diving to bungee jumping to walking down a dark alley with one hundred dollar bills hanging out of his pockets, but he realized his good luck would not allow him to be hurt.

At one point during one of his past bouts of depression he had actually considered trying to commit suicide but he instinctively knew no matter how hard he tried he would never succeed; his good fortune simply would not permit it. He was destined to live a long and healthy live of great wealth; a life he no longer wanted.

As he stepped onto the elaborate brick and stone porch of his enormous mansion, Stephen thought about all he had acquired and about all he had lost and about how foolish and naïve he had been. God, he missed his wife and daughter so much, and no matter how much money or good fortune came his way it would never even begin to make of for their loss.

He inserted his key into the lock on the finely handcrafted front door, and with a click he walked into the darkened hallway. He switched on the overhead hall light, which simultaneously turned on a small lamp on the oak hall table. He knew he should have put the table lamp on a timer but Stephen had no intcrest taking the time to bother with such things. The dense mist of apathy that had taken over his psyche like a creeping fog of malcontention was most likely responsible. It could also have been that he simply found technology to be more of an annoyance than a benefit. This was also the reason why he was able to enter the home without hearing the blaring of an alarm system in desperate need of resetting. He just didn't feel like dealing with the hassles of owning such devices. Besides, he knew he had nothing to worry about from any living being.

Stephen casually approached the hall table and placed the large grocery bag he was carrying on top of the table, then reached into his coat pocket and pulled out a wrinkled lottery ticket and laid it next to the bag. He took off his coat and hung it in the hall closet, deciding to walk down the hall past the living room and out to his kitchen. Perhaps he could make himself something exciting for dinner. He was not much of a cook, but maybe the distraction would be a good thing. He knew he could simply select any one of hundreds of phone numbers in his smart phone and he would be able to order whatever he wanted from wherever he chose any time day or night. If he so desired, he could hop on a plane and fly to France or Italy or even China simply for the purpose of having an interesting meal.

"I think that's about far enough," Stephen heard a gruff voice say from inside the living room as he attempted to pass by the wide arched opening. He looked up and saw a trace of shadowed movement from deep within the darkness. A few seconds later he caught a glimpse of two dark eyes reflected in the light from the hall, along with a flash of something metallic located approximately waist high.

A gun, Stephen thought. There's an intruder in my home and he has a gun. Yet he remained surprisingly calm as if the sight of a weapon pointed in his direction was a daily occurrence, which of course it was not.

It was just that Stephen had realized the intruder, who although intent on something nefarious, might actually prove to be exactly what he was looking for; the answer to his own unending plight. He tried to see back into the gloom to determine what the prowler might look like but could only see the man's pale extended hand; the one holding a very menacing looking pistol.

"You know," the mysterious stranger said, "owning a house like this and not bothering to install a security system is pretty damn stupid, in my opinion."

Stephen didn't reply but stood staring into the darkness. The intruder continued, "I could have simply come up behind you and slit your fool throat if I was so inclined. You are either extremely naïve or very stupid. If you hadn't come home just now I had every intention of robbing you blind. Oh, and for the record, I still plan to do just that." The robber was caught off guard when instead of appearing terrified Stephen shrugged his shoulders as if he didn't care one way or the other. Stephen stood quietly for a few more moments before shaking his head as if disbelieving the strange situation he now found himself in. And then to make matters worse, Stephen chuckled aloud, unable to control himself.

"I don't see what you find so funny," the stranger said with rising indignation and a significant amount of confusion. "In case you haven't noticed, I have a gun here, Einstein. And that means I hold your life in my hands and can end it at any time I choose with the simple pull of this trigger."

Stephen was perfectly aware of the severity of his situation but what the intruder didn't realize was that it was this entire situation that Stephen found so oddly amusing.

After a few more moments of silence, Stephen finally decided to speak up and said with surprising calm, "Yes, I see your gun. And, yes, I can also see it's pointed directly at me. But I think I need to let you in on a little secret. If you truly believe you hold my life in your hands, then you are sadly mistaken, my friend; because you do not. However, if it makes you happy to believe in such fairy tales then by all means go right ahead and shoot." Then Stephen waited a beat expecting to hear the crack of gunfire, feigning nonchalance while all the time hoping against hope that his amazing luck would suddenly fail him and he would be shot and finally reunited with his family. But there was no gunshot.

Although Stephen couldn't see the man's face he was quite certain he must have worn an expression of utter astonishment at this last audacious statement. After all, what sort of madman would so boldly suggest to someone pointing a gun at him that the attacker should pull the trigger? But Stephen knew things, many things that the intruder did not. And even without that knowledge Stephen was fairly certain the man was not even an experienced burglar and certain by the man's actions so far he was not a murderer by nature. Had the intruder been so inclined he would have simply knocked Stephen unconscious or killed him already rather than stopping him and issuing what Stephen was certain was an idle threat.

"No, I didn't think so. I don't believe you're a killer, my new mysterious friend," Stephen said now standing in a surprisingly relaxed pose as if nothing were out of the ordinary.

"Look, buddy," The man replied nervously growing obviously more nervous, "I'm not your friggin' friend. And maybe you're right. Maybe I'm not a killer; at least I may not have been a killer when I walked in here, but that don't mean I can't become one." Although the man was still hidden in the shadows, Stephen could see by the way the gun was fidgeting in the reflective light that the man was getting anxious and uncomfortable. "Look . . . I'm a very desperate man, and desperate men have been known to do things they might not normally consider . . . especially if they are pushed too far. And for your information, you are beginning to push me too far."

Stephen said, "Although you may not believe it, I honestly do know where you're coming from and I understand your situation completely."

The man waved his gun in a menacing manner and replied with frustration, "Understand? Understand? How in the hell could you possibly understand what I'm going through? Look at this place. It's a mansion; a friggin' palace. You're obviously filthy rich and you want for nothing, while every day for me is a struggle just to try to survive."

Stephen insisted, "Look, despite outward appearances, I understand more than you realize. And I can empathize with you. Please, allow me to help you. Just tell me what happened to you to drive you to this. And considering that you plan on robbing me anyway and have already threatened my life once, I think you owe me that much. Wouldn't you agree?"

"What? Agree? Are you insane? I don't owe you a damned thing." The man shouted, "I'm here to take your money and that's all you need to know. That and the fact that if you don't tell me where you have hidden your cash, I'm gonna splatter your guts all over the wall." He lifted the gun shakily and shouted, "And don't think for one second that I won't do it either!"

Stephen tried again to reason with the man using a calm voice. "Easy now, my friend. I have every intention of giving you everything you want and possibly even more than you anticipated. All right? For starters why don't you come over here and look in this grocery bag. You can have everything inside if you want it. Go ahead. Take a look. It's all yours."

"What? Groceries?" The man screamed. "I'm not here to beg for food, you idiot, and I'm not looking for your charity either. I am here to rob you—R-O-B—rob! So give me your money. NOW!"

"Well then," Stephen replied still sounding strangely calm. Then take a look inside the bag and I promise you won't be disappointed.

Furiously, the man waved his gun, ordering Stephen to step aside. Then forgetting himself, the robber stepped out from the shadows and for the first time Stephen got a good look at him. He was a tall, thin, relatively good looking man with dark hair and surprisingly intelligent eyes. Stephen had expected a thug or perhaps at the very least some sort of street-smart tough guy. But what he saw before him was someone who was very much like he had once been. The man was obviously inexperienced in his new chosen profession. Stephen was suddenly filled with excitement at the potential the man offered for him. This man really could be the answer to all of his prayers.

Keeping the gun trained on Stephen, the robber slowly approached the large paper sack and quickly peeked inside, turning his attention immediately back to Stephen. Then he did a double-take; looked back into the bag and momentarily froze with amazement, his eyes growing wide with disbelief. The hand holding the gun began to tremble slightly and for a moment, Stephen worried it might accidently go off. Then realizing the absurdity of his worry he brushed the thought aside.

"What the hell!" The man shouted. "What is all this? Some kind of joke? The bag is full of money. There must be several thousand bucks in cash in here."

"Yeah. I know," Stephen replied. "Based on past experience, I would say maybe twenty or thirty grand give or take a few."

The burglar, whose real name was Thomas Stewart, stared at Stephen for a moment with an expression of perplexity, then a light of recognition appeared on his face. He thought to himself, Oh yeah . . . now I think I get what's going on here. This guy isn't just some rich a-hole who inherited a ton of money. He's a thief; a crook just like me. Then just as quickly Thomas realized that if his would-be victim was a robber he was obviously much more successful at the trade than Thomas had been so far. The house was incredible so there must be more to the man than he originally assumed.

Keeping his gun trained on Stephen Thomas asked, "So what did you do, rob a bank or what?"

Stephen realized the intruder had misunderstood him and apparently had mistaken him for a fellow criminal. He laughed, "I didn't rob anyone. I just found the bag out along the highway, just as you see it there."

Thomas was not going to fall for such a preposterous lie, "Yeah. Right. You mean to try to tell me that you were walking down the street and found a grocery bag full of cash? Just like that?" Thomas snapped his fingers to accentuate his statement. "What do you take me for, some kind of idiot? Nobody has that kind of good luck."

"I do," Stephen replied matter-of-factly. "I have that sort of amazing financial luck all the time. In fact, do you see that lottery ticket I found?"

Thomas looked down at the crumpled ticket. "Yeah, I see it. What about it?"

Stephen replied, "Well, I also found that while I was out walking. And although you interrupted me before I had time to check the website, I'd be willing to bet it is a winner; and not just a winner but a really big winner."

"Uh huh!" Thomas replied with disbelief. "You must take me for a real chump, expecting me to believe this load of crap you're shoveling. Do you have any idea what the odds are of anyone winning big on the lottery, let alone winning with some wrinkled up old discarded ticket you found along the road?"

"The odds are probably astronomical," Stephen admitted. "But nonetheless, I guarantee the ticket will be a major winner. That's just the way things work for me. Look. I don't know exactly what your story is, my friend, but you said you were a desperate man," Stephen continued. "Once I, too, was an equally desperate man. Now I have all of this. But I'm going to venture a guess at your current situation. I am thinking that once you were a fairly successful upper middle class professional earning a good living. Then the economy went bad, you lost your job and you either lost your home or are about to lose it. How am I doing so far?"

Thomas looked at Stephen with shocked surprise, wondering how this stranger could have possibly gotten his story so correct. He had never met the man before but somehow he knew about his job loss and the fact that the bank was about to foreclose on his home. Thomas was unable to reply so he just stood staring, slack-jawed at Stephen and slowly nodded his head in agreement.

"I would also speculate that you have a wife and family and although your wife has stood by you so far, things are getting rough on the home front," Stephen said. "And you're afraid if you do actually lose your home then your wife will leave you and most likely take the kids with her."

This was all so bizarre. Thomas had no idea how this man with his oddly confident manner could know so much about his life.

Stephen continued. "Yep. I think I nailed your situation down perfectly. And although I know you may find this hard to believe, just a few years ago I was in the same boat as you were, or perhaps sinking ship might be a better description, then everything changed for me, overnight."

Finally Thomas found his voice and asked, "Overnight? Not possible! What do you expect me to believe? That you found a magic lamp with a genie who granted you three wishes? What sort of fool do you take me for?"

"Well. It was not exactly like that but something along those lines," Stephen said. "I was like you. I had a wife and daughter but I had lost my job and could not find another. The bill collectors were banging on my door and ringing my phone off the hook. The bank was about to take my home."

"All right," Thomas said. "Suppose I buy into your cockamamie story. Where did all of this come from?" Thomas waved his arm to indicate the opulent surroundings of Stephen's home.

Stephen replied, "Someone offered me the opportunity to change my financial luck and I took it. This was the result. And if you think you'd like to have what I have and more I can arrange that for you as well."

"And why in the hell would you want to do that for someone like me who came here to rob you?" Thomas asked suspiciously. "What is this, some kind of con? Is it some ridiculous get rich pyramid scheme? Look, buddy, I've been approached by all these types before and I'm not about to fall for such crap and head down that particular road to ruin."

"I assure you," Stephen said. "It's not a scheme or business. And although it may seem like I'm doing you a favor, I guarantee you my reasons are purely selfish; I am doing this only for myself. You probably won't believe me, but the truth is that I am tired of all of this. When I was in trouble like you are, I thought money would bring me happiness, but it has not. All it has brought me is sorrow," Stephen said. "You and everyone else might think I should be the happiest man alive but I'm far from it. So the only way for me to truly change my life is to get someone else, such as yourself, to voluntarily take my place."

Thomas asked, "Take your place? What is that supposed to mean?"

Stephen explained, "All this amazing good fortune can only belong to one person at a time. Before me it belonged to another man and before him, someone else. I have no idea how far back in time it goes, but I suspect centuries. The important thing is that I have it now and am offering it to you."

Thomas once again looked perplexed and said, "This is insane. But just assume for a minute that I'm desperate enough to be willing to play along with you. How in the hell do you propose to make this supposed transfer of good luck happen?"

"It's quite simple really." Stephen said, "All you have to do is ask me. If you just tell me you wish you could have all the luck I currently possess and all the money you could ever need and I agree, then it will be yours. What will happen is the good fortune will leave my body and go into yours. And from that moment on you will never want for money again. But you have to be sure this is really what you want. And I have to warn you to be very careful what you wish for, because you just might get it; as I did."

Thomas was sure this stranger was out of his mind; some kind of rich eccentric wacko. And what was that last cryptic statement supposed to mean? "Be careful what you wish for?" What was that all about? The guy was obviously some kind of nut job, Thomas was certain. But as he, himself, had said earlier that he was a desperate man and desperate men tend to do things they normally would never previously have considered. So he decided to play along with the lunatic. The worst case scenario was he might get some cash out of the deal. "Not that it really matters to me, but what is supposed to happen to you if I make this wish and take away all of your good fortune? What will become of you?"

Stephen said, "That's a good question. Here's how it works. When you make your wish, all of my luck will become yours. When the transfer is complete, this house and everything in it will be yours. I'll simply leave and you will never see me again."

"Wait a minute! Hold your horses! I get this now." Thomas said distrustfully. "You're trying to con me into letting you go. Then as soon as you walk out that door you'll go around the corner and call the cops. A few minutes later they'll bust in here and haul my sorry butt off the jail. Well, fat chance, buddy! If you honestly think I'm going to let you walk out the front door like that, then you're crazier than I thought." Thomas raised the gun and pointed it straight at Stephen's chest.

Stephen never flinched or showed the slightest sign of fear. Instead he said, "Then I suppose I have to prove it to you. I have to convince you that what I am saying is true. What do you suppose the odds are of a bullet missing me from your current distance?"

"What?" Thomas asked once again caught off guard, "What the hell are you saying? From this distance, a blind man wouldn't miss. Are you telling me you want me to shoot you from this point blank range? Are you suicidal or what?"

"No, not really," Stephen said. "I have to admit at one time I was but no longer. I also believe even at this close proximity if you shot at me you wouldn't hit me. You have no idea how powerful all of this is. Look, I realize you don't consider yourself the murdering kind, but I assure you if you pull that trigger you won't harm me."

Thomas said, "OK. Wait a minute here. Maybe you're just out of your friggin' mind or something. I don't know. But I have no intention on killing you unless I have no other choice. So I'm not about to pull this trigger just because you say so, OK? How's about this . . . why don't I just take this bag of money and leave?" Things were getting way too weird for Thomas and his gut was telling him to leave immediately.

Stephen retorted, "If you think that will satisfy you then please just take the bag and go. And feel free to take the lottery ticket as well. But I don't think that will be enough for you; I suspect you want more. And if you do really want more, so much more, then I have a better idea. All you have to do is tell me that you wish you had all of my luck and I was left with none of it. If you do than then all the riches you ever imagined will be yours. But the key is, you can't just say the words, you really have to mean them."

For a moment Thomas stood silently staring at Stephen as if studying his expression for signs of deception. There were none. Thomas thought, this guy really believes everything he is saying. In his mind, he thinks he's telling me the truth. Then Thomas suddenly realized that it didn't really matter whether he believed in wishes or good luck himself, because the man standing in front of him most certainly did. And what that meant to Thomas was, if he could convince this strange man he really did believe what he was saying and that he would accept Steven's proposition, then the madman really might be crazy enough to actually sign over his house and all of his money to him. Thomas decided to do his best to gain the man's confidence.

"What is your name?" Thomas asked Stephen, figuring that was as good of a place as any to start.

"Stephen," he replied. "Stephen Albright is my name. And yours? If I may ask."

Thomas hesitated for a moment then decided to be honest with Stephen. If he was going to pull this off he had to be truthful. He said, "My name is Thomas Stewart."

Stephen said, "Very well, Thomas Stewart. May I assume you are considering taking me up on my offer? Are you ready to assume my place and claim you own financial fortune?"

"I am," Thomas replied, but still somewhat warily. He had never dealt with a crazy person before and he had no idea what might happen next. There was also something so very odd about the way this Stephen character was in such a hurry to give away his fortune that for the first time

Thomas actually began to feel apprehensive about everything. Although he was not prone to superstition, something felt not quite right about all of this. He thought of something his father had once told him: "Tommy, if something sounds too good to be true, it probably is."

But Thomas needed to believe Stephen was nothing more than an eccentric crackpot. And since Thomas still held the gun and had it pointed directly at Stephen, there was little the man could do to harm him. Yet he felt something was still a bit wrong with the entire situation. All sorts of internal alarms went off at once, as if warning Thomas to grab the bag of money and flee. But Thomas was convinced that these feelings were unfounded and he decided, Why should he settle for a bag of money when he could have it all? This crazy man was offering him a whole new lease on life.

"OK," Thomas acknowledged. Then he asked, "What should I do? I mean . . . how do I make all of this happen?" He didn't want to screw up what could be a very sweet deal.

Stephen explained, "Just say aloud that you wish you had all of the luck I currently have and that I would no longer have any of it. It's as simple as that. But once again, I have to warn you to make sure you really mean what you are saying and that deep down in the very pit of your soul this is really what you want."

Thomas realized such a declaration would not be a problem for him because he and his family had been struggling just to stay afloat for so many years. Things had gotten about as bad as he felt they could ever get; so bad that he had stooped so low as to try to rob Stephen's home. He even realized that if it had become necessary he really could have murdered the man; shot him in cold blood. That was exactly how bad things had become. Thomas loved his wife and family, and as such would do anything in his power to help them. He would have done anything I if it meant helping his family. So as unbelievable as it might be, what Stephen was offering could be his last chance he had to save his family.

"Yes," Thomas said. "I'll do it." He braced himself for what he was certain would prove to be a major letdown, took a deep breath, and said, "I want what you have. I want all of the luck you possess to leave your body and come into mine. I want your riches. I want your good fortune. And I want you to have none of it any longer."

For a second or so nothing seemed to happen. Then slowly at first Thomas noticed a white sparkling vapor begin to seep from Stephen's body as if every pore of his flesh was emitting the haze. Soon a cloud-like fog hovered above Stephen's head and he swooned a bit on his feet as if the strength had been sucked out of him and looked as if he might pass out.

Then the sparkling mist slowly traveled across the space between the men and surrounded Thomas's body. He felt his skin tingle and the hair on his arms seemed to stand on end as if he were in the middle of an atmosphere charged with electromagnetic energy. Next the vapors entered his own body through his pores and he was filled with a strange, sort of satisfying warmth.

Thomas could see Stephen standing across the room watching him; watching the whole spectacle with calm reservation and what appeared to be a look of relief, as if he had been somehow freed from some horrible curse rather than having just given away a fortune. Once again, Thomas began to sense a deep discomfort as if all of this perceived good luck might suddenly go very bad.

After a few moments the tingling of his flesh stopped as did the deep heat he felt inside. Those sensations were replaced with a sudden feeling of euphoria, the likes of which Thomas had never experienced before. His previous thoughts of concern vanished amid all of his happiness. Thomas realized he had never felt so strong, so positive, and so self-assured in his entire life. He believed he could do no wrong, as if anything he ever attempted would be successful; as if every thought he would ever have would end up being deemed pure genius. Thomas could not comprehend why Stephen would have ever become tired of such feelings or why he would have willingly given up the incredible sensations.

"Open the top drawer of the hall table," Stephen said, still sounding a bit weak from the ordeal. "There are some documents in there for you."

Thomas, still under the positive influence of his new-found euphoria didn't even question why there might be anything in this house specifically meant for him. Instead, he opened the drawer and withdrew what appeared to be a large legal document as well as several smaller documents.

Stephen said, "That top document is a deed to this house and the surrounding land. There are also copies of all of my active financial accounts and investments; or should I say, your investments now."

Still stunned, Thomas opened the top document as was astonished to see the name on the cover sheet change right before his eyes. Stephen Albright began to fade and was simultaneously overwritten with his own name, Thomas Stewart. As he leafed through the remaining documents the same thing happened to each of them. His name was now on every single financial certificate. He saw numbers totaling in the millions flashing by as he skimmed the papers.

"You mean to say it's really true? All of this? Everything? It's all mine?" Thomas asked with utter disbelief.

"Yes," Stephen replied. "Everything; all of the wealth and riches you could ever imagine will be yours for the rest of your life. That is to say unless you choose to offer it to someone else, as I have done with you."

Thomas looked aghast. "And why would I ever want to do that? Just because you were stupid enough to give it all away, doesn't mean I am equally as crazy. This is everything I've ever dreamed about all of my life. Its more wealth than I could spend in several lifetimes. What amazing luck! I'd never give away such an incredible gift. All of my troubles are officially over. My wife, my kids, and I will have everything we ever dreamed of. She won't believe me when I tell her. Speaking of which, I have to call her right now and tell her the good news."

Stephen said nothing. He just looked knowingly with pity as Thomas tucked his gun behind his back and pulled out a cell phone. Thomas's face with filled with so much joy at the thought of telling his family of his new-found fortune. But Stephen stood silently, knowing what was about to happen next.

There were laws that governed the universe; some known by man, others unknown. There were physical laws as well as spiritual and economic laws. One such law, which Stephen knew far too well, stated that there was only so much of everything available and for everything you chose to get you must give up something else. If you, for example, had two hours of spare time available and had to decide between going to dinner or to a movie; if you choose one you must sacrifice the other. This rule was one Thomas was sadly about to learn.

"Jenny? It's me," Thomas said into the phone. Then after a bit of hesitation he said. "Excuse me? Who is this? Where's my wife, and what are you doing with her cell phone?" Then a dark shadow passed across Thomas's face and he replied to the voice on the other end of the line. "Oh my God! Which hospital? Saint Luke's you say? I'll be right there."

Stephen didn't ask what the problem was because it really didn't matter what the particular set of circumstances might be—he understood the result would be the same. He already knew Thomas's wife and family were dead and that the policeman simply hadn't wanted to break the news to Thomas over the phone. It was a similar scenario to that which he, himself had been through several years ago when his own wife and daughter had been killed within a few seconds of his taking ownership of the very same gift.

"That—that was . . . he said . . . he was . . . a police officer," Thomas stammered. "He said there was . . . was an accident. My wife and kids were injured . . ." his voice caught in his throat ". . . and they are on their way to the hospital by ambulance. I had better get right over there."

"If you feel you must," Stephen said.

"Of course I must!" Thomas shouted. "It's my family for Christ's sake. They've been injured. They need me."

Stephen said, "You mean they needed you. And you weren't there, because you were here claiming what was really the most important in your life; money."

Thomas said, "How dare you! Screw you, Stephen. You know that's not true. I was only here trying to take care of my family's future."

"And it appears you did just that. Now your family has no future," Stephen said. "I might as well tell you there's no need to hurry to the hospital. It won't do any good. By the time you get there they will all be dead; that is, if they aren't dead already."

Thomas looked confused and furious, "What? How . . . how can you pretend to know that? What the hell are you talking about?"

Stephen said, "Remember, I warned you to be careful what you wished for. But apparently you were so busy thinking about all of the money you'd have that you didn't think things through. I understand completely, because as I said, I, too, was once as desperate as you."

"But this . . . this thing . . . was supposed to bring me good fortune," Thomas pleaded. "And now you tell me my family is dead. What kind of good luck is that?"

Stephen said, "A simple law of the universe is that you can't have everything. For each thing you choose to have you either voluntarily or involuntarily choose to give up something else. And you have made your choice."

Thomas asked tearfully, "Are you trying to tell me I caused this to happen to my family by choosing to make one stupid wish?"

Stephen said, "I promised you that you would have more money than you could ever spend and you would never have to worry about being injured and killed for all of your natural life. I said you would live a long and healthy life and someday die of natural causes as a very old, very wealthy man. That is what this particular good fortune is about. And now you have all of those things."

"But my wife and my children! How can they be dead?" Thomas shouted as best as his sobbing voice would permit. "What good is all the money in the world if everyone I love is dead?"

"That might have been a good question to ask earlier. I tried to warn you to be careful," Stephen repeated. "But you didn't. And now what was mine is yours." Then Stephen slowly turned to leave.

Thomas shouted, "Where the hell do you think you're going?" He reached around his back and once more brought out the pistol, pointing it menacingly at Stephen.

Stephen replied, "I told you before I was going to leave and so now I'm going to do just that. You have what you came here for and now I'm going to try and start a new life. Maybe if I am truly lucky I will find some semblance of true happiness before I die."

"You bastard! You knew this would happen!" Thomas said accusingly. "You said you had a family once. They probably also died because of this horrible wish; this curse. You tricked me into this devil's bargain and now I'm all alone in the world." He sobbed uncontrollably. "It's all your fault! Don't you dare move another step closer to that door or so help me God I will shoot you!"

"I'm truly sorry about you family," Stephen said, "As I was sorry about my own. In fact I've hated myself every day of my life since I made the same bargain you just made and I'm quite certain you too will be wallowing in misery for many years to come. But that's no longer my problem. It's yours. So if you will excuse me, I will be leaving. Unless you are truly prepared to shoot me, I suggest you just accept your good fortune and make the best of it."

Thomas shouted with insane rage, "Die, you bastard!" Then he pulled the trigger and the room echoed with the deafening blast from his handgun. Stephen was slammed against the wall as a bullet entered his stomach. He involuntarily reached down to the place where he had been shot and his hands came away covered with the blood pouring from his wound.

To Thomas's shock, Stephen didn't cry out or look as if he were in any pain whatsoever. In fact, it looked to Thomas as if the man was happy he had just been mortally wounded, evident by the expression of satisfaction Stephen had on his dying face.

"You . . . you wanted me to shoot you," Thomas said. "That was your plan all along. Oh my God, you actually wanted to die and got me to kill you. You played me the whole time."

Stephen seemed to be staring out into space as if seeing and smiling at something or someone who was invisible to Thomas. Then he slid down the wall landing on his backside on the floor, still sitting and staring joyfully at the same seemingly empty space.

Thomas dropped the gun to the floor then fell to his knees and buried his face in his hands allowing the tears to flow freely. He had been desperate, greedy, and had not listened to the warnings his own subconscious had been giving him. He had been a fool. He now had all the money he could ever imagine, yet like Stephen, he had nothing. He stared at the bloody corpse of Stephen Albright and mumbled, "Be careful what you wish for . . . you just might get it."